RETRIBUTION

FATEFUL JUSTICE BOOK 3

SARA VINDUSKA

ISBN:1673269710

ISBN-13: 978-1673269710

Cover designed by Sweet 'N Spicy Designs *www.sweetnspicydesigns.com*

❀ Created with Vellum

RETRIBUTION

To Sharon- My amazing mother-in-law, fellow wine lover, travel buddy and book lover.

As a former Navy SEAL and bodyguard to one of the world's top Hollywood actors, John Hoyt thought joining the FBI was a logical next step. He never imagined his first case would nearly cost him his life and put him face to face with the one woman he was willing to die for.

Angelina Nobles has spent her career in the FBI living up to the legend of her father. Now, on her most highly publicized case, she's partnered with a man who infuriates and intrigues her like no other has done before.

Can the two put aside their differences long enough to stay alive and solve a complicated case involving a corrupt politician, arson, murder and drugs? And find love in the process?

Danger and intrigue make a powerful aphrodisiac in *Retribution*.

Retribution continues the story of Lash Brogan and his friends. Join them in a world where fate's not fair, but justice and true love are certain.

PROLOGUE

Lash Brogan had a damned good idea why his chief bodyguard had called for the afternoon meeting. He was already working on his second glass of whiskey and handed John Hoyt a cold beer as soon as he walked into Lash's study. Lash sat down in one of the worn leather chairs, motioned Hoyt to the other.

John Hoyt took a long drink of his beer. He'd had it all worked out in his head, what he would say. How much of an honor it had been to work for Lash, how much he appreciated the opportunity Lash had given him, how much he respected the other man. But the words wouldn't come.

Lash gave him a crooked grin, ran a hand through his curly reddish-brown hair. "When are you leaving?" he asked.

Hoyt had too many years of training to show any reaction. Then he smiled and shook his head. "I think you're in the wrong line of work, my friend." He took another drink then leaned forward, elbows on his knees. "And that's part of the problem. I consider you my friend."

Lash finished his whiskey. "We've been through a lot together. And there's no question that I owe my life to you, several times over."

Hoyt gave a rare laugh. "You certainly have proven to be a challenge. Who knew actors could get into so much damned trouble?"

Lash rose and went to the small corner bar to get them each another drink. He turned and raised an eyebrow. "Guess I'm just lucky?"

Hoyt relaxed, knowing no more explanation was needed between the two of them. "Luck of the Irish, my ass," he muttered as he accepted the fresh beer.

"What are you going to do now?" Lash asked, sitting back down.

And that was a damned good question. One Hoyt didn't have the answer to yet. "Not sure. Other than spending a few weeks on a beach somewhere."

"Well, you certainly deserve some time off."

"I haven't talked to Rafe yet, but I think he's ready to take over. He's young, but he's got a good rapport with the guys. And he's proven he can handle himself in difficult situations."

Lash waved a hand. "I'll worry about that later. For now, you stay here and relax. I'll go talk to Lauren and we'll plan something special for dinner."

AFTER DINNER, Lash sat outside on the deck, another glass of whiskey in hand. He loved the peacefulness of his Wyoming ranch, especially in the fall. Despite everything that had happened there, it was his safe haven. His own little piece of heaven. He'd gotten married here. He and his wife Lauren enjoyed the time they spent at their New York City apartment, but this was truly his home.

Here he could be himself. Here he was just Lash Brogan, an Irish immigrant who'd worked his ass off to get where he was. Not the asshole actor most people thought he was. Here there were no reporters. No photographers. No overzealous fans.

Just him and his wife. And a dozen assorted bodyguards and household staff. But even those were carefully handpicked and almost like extended family.

He was glad Hoyt was moving on. He really was. The man was too fucking good at what he did to stay a bodyguard. If not for John Hoyt, Lash really would be dead several times over. No question about it.

That thought produced a shiver and Lash drank deeply, trying to force the memories down. When he closed his eyes, he could still feel the pain of the bullet slamming into his body. He could see the faces of the men he'd killed. Feel the cold water filling his lungs when he'd nearly drowned. See the fear on the faces of the two women he'd loved in this world as they faced death.

He shuddered, shook his head. Focused on the present. Not the past.

The truth was, he had a damned good life. One he truly didn't deserve. He picked up the bottle at his feet and topped off his glass. Drinking while he was in a dark mood wasn't a good idea. He knew that better than most. He sat the full glass down, ran a hand down his face. He heard the sliding glass door open behind him and smiled.

Lauren picked up the glass and took a long drink, then sat down on his lap, lacing her fingers behind his neck.

He pulled her close, breathing in her scent. The dark thoughts disappeared as her lips touched his and everything in his world was right again.

1

John Hoyt dug his feet into the warm sand, drained the last swallow of his Corona, and signaled the waiter for another one. His sharp eyes scanned the crowd of scantily clad women and men, then gazed out at the rolling ocean waves.

Paradise.

He'd made good use of the two weeks he'd been in Cozumel, enjoying the pleasures of a few beautiful women, drinking a lot of ice cold beer, and working on his tan. He sighed. Now he was bored off his ass. A man like him wasn't made to sit around on the beach all day. He just wasn't built that way.

His fresh beer arrived and he drained half of it in one swallow, knowing he'd need it for the phone call it was time to make. He took another deep drink and reluctantly punched the number on his cell phone.

"Calhoun," the familiar voice of the Special Agent in Charge of the Denver field office barked into the phone.

Hoyt thought about hanging up on the FBI agent, but couldn't do it. "It's John Hoyt."

"Hoyt, about goddamn time you called."

"Nice to talk to you, too, Ward."

"Look, there's no point wasting time with chitchat. I know why you called."

Hoyt grunted and thought about hanging up again. "So?" he asked.

"There's a new agent training class starting next week. Your name's on the list."

"I'll be there." Hoyt hung up and rubbed a hand over the stubble on his face, hoping like hell he'd made the right decision.

RAFE BRAEDEN TOOK a deep breath before knocking on his boss's door. It was rare for him to be nervous, but with John Hoyt leaving, he couldn't deny that he wanted the promotion to head of Lash Brogan's security team. He also couldn't deny that he and Lash hadn't gotten off to the best start. He knew he'd proven himself over the last few years. Knew Lash trusted him. But was it enough?

The door opened. He took another deep breath. He was about to find out.

Lash quickly ushered him inside and to the spacious kitchen.

"Drink?" his boss asked.

Rafe shook his head. "I'm good, thanks."

Lash shrugged.

They both took a seat at the breakfast bar.

Lash looked down, then back up again. "I may not remember hiring you, but I'm damned sure glad I did. You've more than lived up to the job, Rafe."

"Thank you, sir."

"Drop the fucking 'sir'. And just to be clear, I'm one hundred percent stone cold sober now and aware that I'm offering you my head of security position. What do you say?"

"I say, hell yes."

Lash grinned. "Good. Now that that's settled, want a drink?"

"Sure," Rafe agreed.

Lash narrowed his eyes. "Whiskey, beer?"

"Never been much of a whiskey drinker."

Lash grabbed a bottle off the counter. "Let's see if we can fix that," he said, pouring two glasses.

An hour later, Rafe stood unsteadily. "Good thing I can walk home," he said, glad he had agreed to live in one of the small cabins on Lash's property.

"You only had one whiskey," Lash said with a laugh, leading him to the front door.

Rafe shrugged. "Never been much of a drinker."

Lash paused, put a hand on his shoulder. "You're in charge now. I trust you. Don't fuck it up."

Rafe looked him in the eye, suddenly feeling very sober. "I won't."

LASH GRINNED as he answered the phone three days later. "How's the tan coming?" he asked.

Hoyt laughed. "Fun in the sun is over. It's back to work now."

"What'd you decide on?" Lash asked.

Hoyt paused.

"Come on, it can't be as bad as becoming a fed."

Hoyt didn't answer.

"Shit," Lash said. "Ward got to you, didn't he?"

"It's not like that."

Lash laughed. "I'm kidding. Kind of. I'm happy for you, but I'm still going to kick my brother-in-law's ass."

Hoyt laughed. "Good luck with that."

"Oh, ye of little faith."

"I have plenty of faith. I trained you. Still, I don't think Lauren would like to clean up the aftermath."

"I'll behave," Lash said.

"Bullshit."

"Seriously, I'm happy for you, man."

"Thanks. I'll be in touch."

Lash laughed and shook his head. He should have seen this coming. Hopefully he wouldn't ever need the services of the FBI again, but at least now he would have two agents he could count on.

"Who was that?" his wife, Lauren, asked coming into the room.

"Hoyt."

"Oh? How's he doing?" she asked.

"Seems your brother talked him into joining the elite ranks of becoming a federal agent." He paused. "You wouldn't happen to know anything about that, now, would you?"

Lauren raised a dark eyebrow, the expression on her face so like that of her older brother, he almost laughed. "Ward may have mentioned it," she said.

"Really?" He stalked towards her, put a hand on her hip and pulled her against his body. "And you didn't think to mention it to me? I may have to punish you for that."

Lash watched his wife's eyes darken with desire. Then she smiled. "I may have also forgotten to mention that Ward is coming for a visit this weekend. You two can hash things out then."

"Now I'm definitely going to have to punish you," he said, with a growl.

Lauren grinned and took his hand, leading him towards the door. "Bring it on," she said, over her shoulder.

WHEN LASH and Lauren were at his ranch in Wyoming, they would invite her brother Ward over for dinner every couple of weeks. As the Special Agent in Charge of the Denver FBI Field Office, he enjoyed being a short flight away from his sister, even though flying wasn't his favorite mode of transportation. He and Lash had a complicated history, starting with when Ward had headed up the investigation into Lash's kidnapping three years ago, through Ward's investigation into a killer on the set of one of Lash's movies, to Lash falling in love with Ward's sister.

It had taken a while for the FBI agent to warm up to the idea of Lash as a brother-in-law, but most of the time now, they enjoyed each other's company.

This probably wouldn't be one of those times, Lash thought as the doorbell rang.

Lauren shot him a warning glance, then opened the front door and gave her brother a hug before ushering him into the dining room.

"Brogan," Ward said, as Lash looked up from the bar where he was pouring two glasses of whiskey.

Lash handed him a drink. "You're lucky I'm still letting you into my house."

"I assume you talked to John?" Ward said as he took the glass.

"You mean my former bodyguard, future FBI Special Agent John Hoyt?" Lash asked with a raised eyebrow.

Ward grunted. "Gotta recruit talent wherever I find it."

Lash took a big drink, then flashed his famous lopsided grin. "I'm glad you did. Much as I hate to admit it, he was way too damned good to hang around here working for me."

"That's the truth," Ward replied, laughing.

Lauren watched them from the doorway, smiling. It never failed to amaze him how much his wife resembled her older brother. They damn well could have been twins. "Well, now that that's out of the way, let's have dinner," she said.

"So, Hoyt graduates next week?" Lash asked as they were served Creme Brûlée for dessert.

"He does."

"How is he doing?"

Ward smiled, put his napkin down. "How do you think?"

"Oh, I'm sure he's the best in his class."

"No one's even fucking close," Ward confirmed.

"Good," Lash replied. "When is the graduation ceremony?"

Ward gave him a hard look. "You need to stay away. No offense."

"You ashamed of me?"

"You know it's not that. But your . . . status sometimes gets in the way."

"I'm married to your sister."

"No shit. But having your name associated with my newest recruit is a recipe for disaster. His name and picture would be all over the news. Which would rule out my ever using him undercover."

"I get it."

"Then stay the fuck behind the scenes."

Lash raised his hands. "You know me."

"That's what I'm afraid of."

Lash's face sobered. "Seriously. I would never put you or John at risk."

Ward nodded. "I know."

Lash put a hand on his shoulder. "We'll have a hell of a party here afterwards."

HOYT KNEW he'd make a good federal agent. It wouldn't really be all that much different from what he'd done in the military. He could fit in anywhere. He wasn't so good at personal relationships, but he could fake it with the best of them.

And he'd enjoyed his time at the academy. It had been an intense few months, that was for sure. A lot of the training he'd already been proficient at: firearms training, Emergency Vehicle Operation Training, training on terrorism and the importance of working informants, physical fitness. It was all second nature to him already after the years he'd spent as a Navy SEAL.

He had been pleasantly surprised at how realistic Hogan's Alley had been. It really was a self-contained city with a hotel, drug store, bank, and private residences where new agents could actually work a case, plan an arrest, and execute it start to finish.

Now he tossed and turned in his narrow bed at the academy dormitory. Tomorrow he graduated. He'd be sworn in and get his badge. He was looking forward to the new challenges.

Like the other new agents in his class, he'd filled in his 'wishlist' of where he wanted his first assignment to be. As the recipient of this class's Director's Leadership Award, he was pretty much guaranteed his first choice. Between that and Ward throwing his weight around, he was virtually guaranteed a spot at the Denver field office.

He smiled as the first light of dawn crept through the window.

Working for Lash had been a nice break. He'd been ready for a slower pace after his years in the SEALs. Not that being Lash Brogan's bodyguard had turned out to be a walk in the park, but he'd grown increasingly restless as the years went on.

It wasn't like he had a god complex or was out to save the world, but the idea of continuing to make a difference, to put the bad guys out of commission . . . well, he was more than ready to spend the rest of his days doing exactly that.

2

Two weeks later, Hoyt looked around his new office. It wasn't anything special, looked like a typical mid-level office building. One of thousands in the city of Denver, Colorado.

He looked down at his pressed khaki pants and blue button-down shirt and wondered what the hell he was doing there. He didn't belong in an office. Yet, here he was.

Now that the intensity of the training was over, he worried that the day-to-day reality of his new job would be boring as hell. Of course, that was what he'd thought when he'd first taken the job working for Lash Brogan. And almost from day one, that job had been anything but boring.

As promised, Lash had thrown one hell of a graduation bash for him. It had been strange being around the man he'd been paid to protect for so long and not being on duty. Whiskey had flowed all night and it had been good to hang out with the guys on the security team one more time. He'd kept a respectable distance from Ward, seeing as how the guy was now his boss.

Now, he just hoped he'd get an assignment soon. He didn't think he could stand being cooped up for long. It felt suffocating already. Joining the FBI had seemed like a logical step after his military and bodyguard careers, but maybe he'd been wrong. Maybe he'd made a huge mistake.

He checked his watch. He had a briefing with Ward in an hour. Hopefully he'd get his first assignment then. He hadn't even bothered unpacking his new apartment a few blocks from the office. He just wanted to get to work and do something.

FBI Special Agent Angelina Nobles knocked softly on her SAC's door.

"Come in," Special Agent in Charge Ward Calhoun commanded.

"You wanted to see me, sir?"

"Sit," he said, gesturing at a chair in front of his desk.

She took a seat. And waited. Despite her best efforts, her hands started sweating. Even silent, her boss could be intimidating as hell. He definitely had the tall, dark and broody thing going on. Though probably somewhere in his forties, she had no doubt he could still kick most of the younger agents asses without breaking a sweat.

The continuing silence unnerved her, made her question yet again her career choice.

She knew she was a good agent, that she'd been assigned based on her own reputation, not that of her father, the retired FBI Executive Assistant Director of the Intelligence Branch, and somewhat of a legend in the bureau. But the doubts were always there in the back of her mind, despite her own successful track record as an agent.

Ward finally looked up from the mess of paperwork on his desk. "I've got a new assignment for you." He paused. "I'll be honest, it's going to be pretty high profile and probably a long and complex case."

Ang sat up. She'd been waiting for something like this to prove herself and get out of her father's shadow. "Sounds good to me, sir," she said.

"Once your partner gets here, we'll go over the details."

"Agent Shuman?" she asked. They'd been partners on a case a few months ago and had worked well together.

Ward shook his head. "I have someone else in mind."

Just then, a knock sounded on the door, and Ang's new partner entered.

Ang looked him up and down, from his close-cropped blond hair to his shiny brown dress shoes. He wasn't a big man, average height, slender but well-muscled. The way he carried himself and the underlying hard edge screamed ex-military of some kind. He was attractive, but not overly so. She'd definitely never seen him around the office before.

She stood and extended her hand. "I don't think we've met yet. I'm Special Agent Angelina Nobles."

The man shook her hand with a firm grip. "Agent John Hoyt."

Once they'd both taken a seat, Ward passed them each a folder. "I'll give you both a minute to skim the file."

Ang glanced up at Ward quickly when she read the name of who they'd be investigating. His face gave nothing away. She looked back down and continued reading. She'd never met Senator David Westmoreland, but she'd seen him plenty of times, in person and on TV. She never would have expected the charismatic senator to be involved in illegal activities, including drug smuggling. But the black and white pages in front of her told an entirely different and very disturbing story. There were too many questionable connections with drug dealers and prostitution rings.

Despite the excitement of his first case, Hoyt wasn't thrilled about being partnered with a woman. He could see Ward's apparent confidence in her, but he had his reservations. In fairness, he'd only worked with men during his time in the military and in the bodyguard business. He knew he needed to remember that and keep an open mind.

But that had all gone out the window when he saw Agent Nobles for the first time. She was tiny. She was attractive, no doubt about that, long shiny blond hair pulled into a sensible ponytail, wearing a nicely tailored suit that hugged her subtle curves. But she was so small. Maybe 5' 2", a hundred pounds tops. How in the hell could he count on her to back him up?

And he knew he'd been cold to her, he admitted to himself as he walked out the door after the briefing. He hadn't said one word to her after their brief introduction. But he couldn't exactly see her having his back in a life-or-death situation. It wasn't a big deal, though. He was comfortable on his own, and while he may have a partner in name, she certainly wasn't one he was going to count on when his life was at stake. And a case like this could definitely go bad fast.

Ang watched her new partner walk out the door without a second glance at her. She collected her things, said goodnight to her boss, and walked out of his office with her head held high.

She wondered if her partner had transferred in from another office or if he was brand new from the academy. Neither he nor their boss had bothered to explain. All she knew was that her new partner seemed like a jerk.

She shook her head. If Agent Hoyt didn't like being partnered with her, then that was his own damned problem. She'd get the job done with or without him.

Ward smiled as he watched the two agents leave his office. Their body language was screaming attraction. They were civil to each other, but didn't seem happy about being partners.

This was going to be interesting. If they could set aside their differences, those two had the potential to be one of the best partnerships he'd seen in all his years with the bureau.

Of course, there was always the chance it could blow up in his face, but Ward doubted that. His instincts were rarely off the mark and he doubted they would be now.

Ward liked that Hoyt knew how to handle himself under pressure in high profile situations. He'd seen that with his own eyes. And Agent Nobles needed to be tested. She'd done well in her assignments so far, but they had all been walks in the park compared to what this case would be. It would be interesting to see if she lived up to the reputation of her father. He was willing to bet that she did.

3

Two days later, Hoyt met Agent Nobles in the parking lot of the field office at 8 a.m. *At least she was on time,* he thought as they both parked and made their way to the bureau car they'd be taking to Casper, Wyoming where Senator Westmoreland lived when he wasn't in Washington, DC. Hoyt was surprised to see she was dressed casually in jeans and a sweatshirt like he was, her hair pulled back into a tight ponytail.

Having acquired the car keys from Ward the night before, Hoyt unlocked the brown Chevy Impala and stowed their bags in the trunk. Agent Nobles raised an eyebrow as Hoyt rounded the car and opened the passenger door for her. "Thank you," she said.

Hoyt didn't respond.

"Mind if we stop for coffee?" she asked as he pulled out of the parking lot.

Hoyt had been up since four, had already worked out and downed two cups of coffee. But it *was* over a four hour drive to Casper. More caffeine couldn't hurt.

He pulled into the next coffee shop with a drive through he saw. He ordered a tall black coffee, surprised for the second time that morning when Nobles asked for the same. He'd fully expected her to request a caramel mocha almond milk something or other.

They drank their coffee and drove in silence, which suited Hoyt just fine.

When she'd finished her coffee, Nobles unbuckled her seatbelt, leaned into the backseat, and started pulling files out of her briefcase.

Hoyt fought to keep his eyes on the road in front of him and not on his new partner's jean clad ass as she bent over next to him.

"Got it," she said, moving back into her seat and buckling back up. She opened the file. "Figured we could at least talk about a game plan while we drove."

"Sounds good," Hoyt said. At least she hadn't tried to start the twenty questions 'let's get to know each other game' like most women. Surprise number three.

"An officer with the Casper police department first contacted our local Resident Agency four months ago when an informant heard whisperings about the senator's involvement in a recent increase in drug shipments in the area.

"The senator recently made several large purchases, including a brand new Mercedes SUV and a condo in Jackson Hole. His wife's a high school teacher and even with his salary, they're living way outside their means."

Hoyt grunted in response.

"We're scheduled to meet with the agents at the Casper Resident Agency at nine tomorrow morning. They'll brief us on what they have so far. Even though it's their area, the agent in charge is new and they're comfortable with us taking the lead," she continued.

That sounded just fine to Hoyt. He smoothly maneuvered the car around a slow moving minivan and focused on the open road in front of them.

HOYT PULLED into the hotel parking lot exactly four hours after they'd left. It was a decent hotel with an attached restaurant and bar, not fancy, but not a dump either. Just like the bureau car he'd driven there. And the building his office was in. Like the clothes most of the agents wore. He had no idea what that said about his new career choice.

He scanned the half-empty parking lot, then the interior of the hotel as they made their way to the front desk, pleased that Agent Nobles was doing the same. She had good situational awareness, he'd give her that.

After getting their room keycards, his for the fourth floor, hers for the second, they headed for the elevator.

"I don't know about you, but I could sure use a drink. Want to meet in the bar in fifteen minutes?" she asked.

Surprise number four. "Sure," he said, because he couldn't think of a reason to turn her down and because a drink sounded damned good.

ANG GOT to the bar before Hoyt. It was still mostly empty that early in the day. She ordered a glass of white wine, took a long swallow, and sighed with pleasure. She hoped over a few drinks she could get to know something about her new partner. Normally they didn't give new agents a high profile case like this, but she supposed with Hoyt's apparent military background and the support of Agent Calhoun, he was the right man for the job. There would be a lot of pressure to end this case quickly. But she wanted to know more about who she'd be working with.

Ten minutes later, Hoyt made his was towards her, leaned against the bar, nodded hello, then ordered a beer.

Ang kept sipping her wine. The strong silent type of man usually annoyed the hell out of her, but it worked for Hoyt. Of course, if they were going to work together, they would have to talk to each other.

"Have you been here in Casper before?" she asked.

He shook his head. "You?"

"No."

They finished their drinks quickly in silence, ordered refills.

"Let's grab a table. Order some food," Hoyt suggested.

"Sounds good," Ang said, following him across the room with their fresh drinks.

Hoyt led the way to a table in the corner of the still mostly empty restaurant. A waitress followed them over with a notepad. He ordered a burger and Agent Nobles ordered a salad. Not a surprise.

He could tell his new partner wanted to talk. It was so much easier working with guys. He knew he was attractive enough that he'd never lacked for female companionship when he wanted it, but he avoided relationships like the plague. And he'd never had a female friend or partner. They'd already talked about the case on the drive, they had a plan of attack for tomorrow, so he really had no idea what to say to her.

"What did you do before joining the bureau? Military, right?" she asked after they'd eaten.

He took a drink, didn't answer.

"How long have you been in the bureau? Did you transfer in from somewhere?"

"Why all the questions?" Hoyt finally asked, trying hard to keep the annoyance out of his voice.

"I'm just trying to learn a little about who I'm working with."

His knee brushed against hers under the table and he felt a spark of electricity surge through his body. And that was a definite surprise. An unwanted one.

She cleared her throat and shifted in the booth. She'd felt it, too.

"This is my first assignment," he said quietly.

"How do you know Agent Calhoun?" she asked.

"I met him when I was doing security." He stopped there, not wanting to get into the details of his past. They didn't matter and he sure as hell didn't want to talk about them with her.

"You must have done something to impress him," she pressed on. "Ward Calhoun doesn't exactly impress easily."

Hoyt shrugged, wishing like hell that she'd just drop the conversation. "Guess so."

"You're not going to tell me?"

He finished his beer. "It doesn't matter. I got the job because of what I can do, not who I know. What's with the third degree?" Hoyt asked. A defensive edge had crept into his voice.

"I didn't mean to offend you." She of all people should have known better than to say something like that. This was not how she wanted their new partnership to start out.

"It's fine." Hoyt looked at his watch. "It's been a long day, let's get settled in. I'll see you in the morning."

Ang watched him walk away, trying very hard not to notice his very nice ass, then finished her own drink. *Damn, what the hell was that all about?*

It would be so much easier to do the job if they could at least be civil to each other. She sighed. As long as he pulled his own weight, they would be fine.

BACK IN HER HOTEL ROOM, Ang unpacked her suitcase and started a bath. When the tub was full, she eased down into the steaming, fragrant bath water, feeling the heat seep into her knotted muscles. The one luxury she never traveled without was her favorite lavender bubble bath.

She breathed in, taking the calming scent deep into her lungs, then slowly exhaled.

The stress was getting to her and they hadn't even started to work the case yet. This was her biggest, most publicized case in her two years with the bureau and she had to be saddled with a newcomer. Ward obviously thought highly of him, but Special Agent John Hoyt struck her as a bit of a loose cannon. She'd have to look into his background since he didn't seem inclined to share it with her. She wanted to know exactly who she'd be working with. She just wished she'd had time to do that before they'd had to leave for Casper.

Whatever his deal was, she was not going to let it interfere with her doing her job. This was the kind of case that could really solidify her career.

She sighed and closed her eyes. It wasn't easy living up to a legend. Her father hadn't been surprised that his only child wanted to follow in his footsteps. But they were some pretty big footsteps. It was a lot to live up to, but she was determined to prove herself.

She couldn't let Agent Hoyt be a distraction. She'd just have to ignore the underlying sexual current between them. He wasn't even that attractive, she told herself, but there was something almost primal about him, in the way he carried himself. He wasn't a big guy, but gave off a definite 'you don't want to fuck with me' vibe.

She eased deeper into the warm water. The sooner this case was over and she never had to see Agent John Hoyt and his nice ass again, the better.

4

Casper Fire Department Captain Edmund Newkirk took the evidence bag from the 8th Street fire out of his desk. He knew he was breaking policy at the very least, and the law at the most, by not turning the bag over to the cops. He had a good relationship with the police chief, but he didn't fully trust the other man. Not with something like this.

It had been a bad scene. Complete with the burned up body of a dead prostitute. It was obviously arson, the fire set by a complete amateur who didn't know how to cover his tracks, or hadn't bothered to try. The question was why.

He turned the charred business card over in his hand. It could be nothing. But the person whose name was embossed on the card would have had no business being in that kind of neighborhood. He told himself he was just following up on a lead as he punched in the numbers on the card. It would probably lead nowhere anyway.

But, he'd heard whispered rumors about the man, allegations of illegal dealings. If that was the case, there might be something in this for Ed.

"Senator Westmoreland's office," a peppy female voice answered promptly on the second ring.

"This is Captain Edmund Newkirk with the Casper Fire Department. I need to speak with the senator."

"I'm sorry, the senator is not available. Can I leave a message for him?"

"I think he'll take my call. It's official business about the fire on 8th Street."

"One moment, please."

Ed tried to not get annoyed as the minutes he was on hold ticked by.

Finally, the irritating Muzak stopped and a deep voice came on the line. "This is Senator Westmoreland. What can I do for the fire department?"

"I won't waste much of your time, senator, but I wanted to let you know we found one of your business cards at the 8th Street fire." He paused. "The one with the dead prostitute."

There was a full minute of silence on the other end. "Have you mentioned this to anyone else?"

"No, sir. I believe in going straight to the source."

"That's a smart man." The senator paused. "Due to my job, it would be very detrimental to a lot of people and to this city if my name were mentioned in conjunction with something like this. You understand."

"I agree, senator. That's why I called."

"So I can trust you to keep this between the two of us?"

"You can, sir."

"Let's just call this fire an accident, District Chief Newkirk."

Ed should say no. He knew he should say no, that it was wrong on so many levels. And yet, it would take years to work his way up to district chief. All he had to do was look the other way this one time.

He thought of the new boat he'd been wanting to buy but couldn't afford on his current salary. Then there was the vacation in Hawaii he'd promised his wife.

And he didn't *really* know beyond a shadow of a doubt that Senator Westmoreland was involved in the death or the fire.

"Senator, what we have here is just a tragic accident," he said.

Senator Westmoreland smiled in his plush ninth floor office across town. "I agree. And I must say, you have a bright future ahead of you, Edmund."

Westmoreland hung up the phone and cursed. He knew he'd been careless with that filthy whore. He hadn't expected her neck to be that fragile. And starting the fire hadn't been his smartest move, but it had seemed like a good idea at the time. And of course he'd worn a condom, so even if they did an autopsy there would be no DNA evidence to link him to the scene.

Damned business card must have slipped out of his pocket. He shook his head.

But it might not be a total loss. The new development with Chief Newkirk could be very valuable. You never knew when it would come in handy to have someone in that position in his pocket.

He unlocked the bottom drawer of his desk. Pouring a small amount of the white powder on the mirror, he breathed it in, felt the euphoric rush.

He hadn't gotten to where he was in life by playing by the rules. He damned sure wasn't going to start now.

ACROSS TOWN, on the way to the Casper Resident Agency, Hoyt pulled into a drive up coffee stand a few blocks from the hotel. "Figured we could use something better than crappy hotel coffee," he said with just a hint of a grin.

Ang smiled back. Hoyt hadn't said a word when she'd joined him at a small table in the breakfast room at the hotel earlier. Maybe there was hope for them as partners yet.

Fifteen minutes later, they pulled into the parking lot of the small FBI field office.

Hoyt opened the door for Ang and they were immediately greeted by a harried looking man.

"I'm Special Agent Josh Sanderson," the man said, running a hand through his too long blond hair.

"Agents Hoyt and Nobles," Hoyt said.

Sanderson led them down a narrow hallway and into a small conference room.

After they'd all taken a seat, Sanderson cleared his throat. "Thank you both for coming. I apologize for our lack of organization. There's only five of us here. Our former agent in charge was recently killed in a car accident. I took over a week ago and we've been scrambling to catch up and get another agent hired."

"I'm sorry to hear that. We've looked over your notes and we're happy to take the lead," Hoyt said.

Sanderson nodded. "Thank you."

"What's your biggest need from us?" Hoyt asked.

"We're a small office, so we don't have enough manpower for effective surveillance. You guys aren't known around here, so that will be a huge help."

"Done," Hoyt said.

"What kind of cooperation can we expect from the local cops?" Ang asked.

"Unfortunately, not much," Sanderson replied. "The cop that originally contacted the FBI isn't with the department anymore, he just up and left town. My predecessor contacted the police chief as soon as he got wind of the senator's activities, but the chief brushed him off. More than likely, he's on the senator's payroll. Politics here are a fucking shit show."

"The cop that called it in, has anyone spoken with him recently?" Hoyt asked.

"I tried. He said he was leaving the country and hung up on me. Good luck finding him," Sanderson said.

"Ok," Hoyt said. "So we can't count on the cops to back us up. Anything else we should know about?"

Sanderson shook his head. "Obviously we have to treat this one very carefully. You've got all the information we have. There's an empty office down the hall that's yours to use. Coffee's in the break room two doors down. And I'm available 24/7, whatever you need."

They all shook hands, then Hoyt and Ang headed to their temporary office.

"So, we're basically on our own," she said after they were out of
Agent Sanderson's earshot.

"Yep," Hoyt agreed, but didn't add that he preferred it that way.

5

First thing the following morning, Hoyt and Ang drove across town to the Casper police station.

The Casper RA had kept the investigation quiet for a long time, and that tactic hadn't exactly paid off yet. Hoyt wanted to shake things up.

"How do you want to play this?" Ang asked as they got out of the car. "Good cop, bad cop?" she asked with a smile.

Hoyt fought back a laugh. Then fought back a very dirty image of Ang playing a dirty cop. *Where the hell had that come from?* He cleared his throat. "We go in and act like we know every one of Chief Delaney's dirty little secrets."

"Okay," Ang said, falling into step next to Hoyt as they entered the police station.

They both took out their badges. "FBI Agents Hoyt and Nobles to see Chief Delaney," Hoyt said to the young female officer at the front desk.

"He's expecting you," the officer said, standing. "Follow me, please."

They followed the officer down the hall and were met at the office door by the chief.

The Casper police chief appeared to be about fifty, with close-cropped salt and pepper hair. He looked to be in good shape for his age. He extended his hand. "Agents," he said without a smile.

He ushered them into his office after brief introductions.

After Hoyt and Ang had taken seats across the desk from him, the chief crossed his arms across his chest and studied them. The desk was spotless, Hoyt noticed. Not a folder or stray Post-it note or even a pen. *Never trust a guy with too clean of a desk*, he thought.

"How can I help the FBI today?" Chief Delaney asked with a raised eyebrow.

"As you probably know, we're here aiding the local resident agency with their investigation into Senator Westmoreland," Hoyt said.

"Which is a complete waste of time, if you ask me," Chief Delaney said.

"Why do you say that?" Hoyt asked.

Delaney sat forward. "Because the senator has an exemplary record. Because he's a great man who's done more for this state and this country than most men could ever dream of. You're barking up the wrong tree, agents."

"Spoken like a man who's in the senator's back pocket," Hoyt said, leaning back in his chair.

Delaney's face reddened. "Whatever the hell it is you think you know, you're wrong," he spat out.

"Guess we'll see about that," Hoyt said, standing up. "If I were you, I wouldn't plan on leaving town anytime soon."

"Get the fuck out of my office," Delaney shouted, lurching out of his chair.

"See you around," Hoyt said as he turned his back on the chief.

Ang followed Hoyt again on the way out of the station. He didn't speak, just stalked across the parking lot to the car. Damned if watching him take charge like that didn't turn her on.

Once they were on the road back to the RA she turned towards him. "That was fun," she said.

Hoyt grunted. "Guy's a fucking asshole."

"But is he guilty?"

"No doubt about it. At the very least, he's being paid to look the other way. We just have to prove it."

Ang didn't respond, just leaned back in her seat.

Hoyt used the silence to think about the police chief. He had instantly disliked the man. The guy was smooth, no doubt about it. But he was also a liar. No matter how good you were, there was no way to avoid the body's subtle signs of dishonesty if you knew where to look.

And Police Chief Delaney was a liar. Hoyt would bet his life on it.

BACK AT THE RA, they headed straight for Agent Sanderson's office.

"How did it go?" Sanderson asked, standing up from his very messy desk.

"He won't admit it, but he's guilty as hell," Hoyt said.

Sanderson couldn't help but notice the heated look in Agent Nobles eyes as she looked at Agent Hoyt. *Interesting.* Hopefully the guy knew what he was doing because getting involved with your partner could easily spell disaster. And the end of careers.

But it wasn't his business. And the truth was, he liked Hoyt's direct, no bullshit approach.

Sanderson was still adjusting to the challenges of being in an office instead of out in the field. The former SAC in charge of their office had been a good man, but he'd been conservative as hell, had always wanted to play it safe. Now that he was in charge, Sanderson had to admit it was nice to have an outsider here to play the bad guy. Especially while he was still figuring out his new role in the organization and the community.

"What do we know about the senator's employees?" Hoyt asked.

Sanderson shrugged. "Not much that isn't in the file."

"What about the senator's aide, Sean Alston? He can't work that close with the senator and not know something," Ang said.

"He never returned our calls," Sanderson said.

Hoyt grinned. "Sounds like we need to pay him a visit."

"Try to be a little discreet," Sanderson said.

"I'll play the situation how it needs to be played."

A muscle in Sanderson's jaw twitched. Then he smiled. "Have at it, Agent Hoyt. Let's see what you can do."

TEN MINUTES LATER, Hoyt and Ang were parked outside the senator's office.

"Aren't we going in?" Ang asked.

"Let's wait. Catch him off guard when he leaves for lunch."

Sean Alston left the building at exactly five minutes after noon. He crossed the street and headed towards a deli the next block over.

Hoyt and Ang exited the car and and kept pace half a block behind the senator's aide.

"Let's give him a few minutes to get comfortable," Hoyt said as they paused outside the deli.

Four minutes later, Hoyt nodded and opened the door.

They moved across the deli, stood in front of the table where the senator's aide sat.

"Who the hell are you?" Alston asked, scooting his chair back.

"Relax," Hoyt said when Alston started to stand. He pulled out his badge. "Sorry to interrupt your lunch, but we've got a few questions for you."

Alston dropped his sandwich, wiped his hands on a napkin. "I don't have anything to say to you."

"Really?" Hoyt asked. "Why do I find that hard to believe?"

Alston stood. "Excuse me. I seem to have lost my appetite."

Hoyt watched the aide hurry out of the restaurant. "Hmm. And I'm suddenly hungry," he said, sitting down at the deserted table, picking up the menu.

Ang raised an eyebrow. "That was you being discreet?"

"What?" He paused. "We need to eat and we've got some time to kill. We can trail Alston when he leaves work, see if we shook anything up."

. . .

THE LATIN DANCE music pounded around them. Lights flashed on the dance floor and couples spun and came together again in perfect rhythm.

They'd followed Senator Westmoreland's aide that evening after he'd left the office and had ended up at a club across town. Sean Alston had just left with a woman he'd been hitting on at the bar. They had both been tipsy and all over each other. No point following him any further tonight, it was a dead end. Ang knew they should head back to the hotel, get some sleep. But she was fascinated by the couples on the dance floor.

"God, I wish I could dance like that," she said in awe.

Hoyt gave her a sideways glance.

"What? You don't dance at all, I suppose. You really should loosen up sometimes, Hoyt."

Before she could utter a word of protest, he had grabbed her by the hand and swept her onto the center of the dance floor. "Follow my lead," he said, gracefully twirling her around.

After a few awkward steps she relaxed and let her body flow with the beat of the music. She felt the heat of Hoyt's hard body against hers, felt the music pulsing through her, and let herself get lost in the sensations as they circled around the dance floor.

Sweat dripped into her eyes as they spun around the other couples. She melted into him as he pulled her even closer.

The music stopped and she looked in awe at Hoyt as he led the way back to the bar. "Where did you learn to dance like that?" she asked as he handed her a beer.

"I spent six months in Mexico. The local senoritas loved teaching us gringos how to dance," he said with a smile.

"Among other things, I'm sure."

He smiled noncommittally and rubbed the cold bottle across his forehead.

Two hours and several dances later, he walked her to her hotel room. "We've got a conference call with Ward at 10 a.m.," he said as she unlocked the door.

She couldn't look at him. The heat of his presence next to her was already making her ache deep inside. "I'll meet you in the lobby at nine for breakfast," she said as she stepped inside her room.

She turned back around, couldn't help herself. "And Hoyt, thanks for the dance," she said with a wink.

Hoyt nodded as she shut the door and tried to get his body under control before he walked back to his room and the cold shower that waited for him.

ANG LEANED against the door after Hoyt left. It had taken all of her willpower to not grab him and pull him into her room. Of all the men in the world, she had to be attracted to her partner. If anyone had told her how this man would leave her needy and aching for him when they'd first met, she'd have told them they were batshit crazy.

Now look at her. Practically melting into a puddle at the man's feet.

She shook her head, pushed off the door. It must have been the dance. The sensual music would get to anyone. And it had been a while since she'd had a lover. Even longer since she'd had one that was any good.

But as she lay in bed later that night, it was thoughts of John Hoyt that filled her mind, keeping her awake. She'd seen a different side of him tonight. One she doubted he let many people see. It was a side she'd like to see more of. Much more.

Her hand drifted down to her breast, imagining it was Hoyt's hand caressing her. Her other hand moved lower, to where she ached with need. What kind of a lover would Special Agent John Hoyt be? Gentle and thorough? Fast and rough?

She closed her eyes, imagined him taking her hard and fast.

6

Hoyt couldn't stand the ache he felt every time Ang was near, which was damn near every minute of the day. Then there were the graphic images of her that kept him awake late at night. It had gotten worse since they'd danced together at the club two nights ago. He couldn't stop thinking about how the small curves of her body felt under his hands. And he couldn't work like this. Maybe if he had her, just once, the ache would go away and he would be able to function again.

He hesitated outside the door to her room. It was the middle of the night. She was his partner. This might be the dumbest fucking thing he'd ever done. But he couldn't stop his hand from knocking on her door. *Just this once*, he promised himself.

"I couldn't sleep," he said, his voice thick when she opened the door. Her heavy blond hair was down, her face bare. She was wearing a red and gold silk kimono wrapped tightly around her narrow waist and he imagined the skin underneath it was just as soft and smooth as the silk that covered it.

Ang gave him a smoldering look that said she knew exactly why he was there. "So," her lips curved into a sly grin, "do you want to just drop down on the floor and go for it, or should we order a bottle of wine first?"

"Dammit, that's not why I'm here."

"The hell it isn't," she challenged, holding his gaze.

"I just . . ." he paused as she loosened her kimono, giving him just a glimpse of naked thigh.

"I admit, I have noticed a certain chemistry between us and I *am* curious," she said with a raised eyebrow.

Hoyt muttered a curse under his breath as she turned and walked towards the bedroom, letting the silk slide off her shoulders and flutter to the ground. She stopped in the doorway and turned. "Well, are you coming?" she asked over a bare shoulder.

Like he had a choice. He stood where he was for a moment, took a breath, then forced his legs to move forward.

She was waiting, just inside the doorway. And damn, was she beautiful, standing naked, her pale skin highlighted by the moonlight streaming through the window.

He was so hard, he didn't think he could walk.

"Well," she said. "Let's get you out of those clothes."

He grinned as she stalked towards him.

As she unbuttoned his shirt, he claimed her mouth.

She ran her hands down his chest, then unbuttoned his pants.

Damned if a woman taking what she wanted didn't turn him on.

When she took him in her hands, he groaned and pushed her down on the bed. She wrapped her legs tight around his waist as he entered her.

Sweet Jesus, nothing had ever felt so good, he thought as he pushed deep into her.

She closed her eyes, gripped his hips, urging him even deeper.

There was no talk, no sweet declarations, no promises. Just pure animalistic passion. Just the way he liked it. He lifted her hips higher and she moaned softly.

As soon as he felt her muscles start clenching around him, he followed, the orgasm blocking out all sights and sounds around him.

. . .

HE WOKE up in the middle of the night to her taut, compact body teasing him and was instantly hard again.

"I can't seem to get you out of my system," he said breathlessly as her hand caressed his back.

"Maybe we should keep trying," she said, squeezing his ass.

He rolled back on top of her. She was already wet and ready for him. He let out a low groan as he entered her.

The second time was even more intense than the first.

ANG WOKE up as the sun rose and turned to find Hoyt awake and studying her. She couldn't read the expression on his face. "Hi," she said.

Hoyt smiled and for the first time since she'd known him, he looked almost gentle, his face totally relaxed. "I should be exhausted, but I guess we're both wide awake," she murmured.

"Mmm hmm," he answered, then leaned back against the headboard and closed his eyes, looking relaxed and sated.

Her gaze fell to his torso. She'd felt the raised scars on his shoulder and chest the night before, but in the early morning light they looked harsh against his otherwise flawless skin. Bullet wounds. She reached out and touched them gently. "These look like they were nasty."

Hoyt opened his eyes, his face serious now. "They were no fun," he said, still remembering the searing pain as the bullets hit, the weeks spent in the hospital recovering.

"How'd you get them?"

He sighed. "When I was working security."

She raised her eyebrows. "Oh, you took a bullet for someone."

"I guess you could say that."

"Anyone famous?" she asked, intrigued now, rolling onto her side.

"Yeah, he's famous," Hoyt answered in a gruff voice.

"Who?"

He didn't answer.

"Who?" she asked again. She raised her eyebrows, "I can find out, you know."

"Lash Brogan."

Yeah, you didn't get much more famous than that, she thought thinking of the world renowned Irish actor. "Lash Brogan? Oh my God . . . the shootout at his ranch. You were there."

"Yeah, I was there." His eyes were hard now.

"I didn't know," she said softly

"How could you?"

"That's how you met Ward. He was the lead agent on the case, and now his sister's married to Lash," she said, sitting up.

Hoyt got out of bed. "I'm not talking about this anymore."

She admired his body as he pulled on his jeans. "And the one on your leg?"

"A souvenir from my time in the SEALs. Now, are you done interrogating me?"

She narrowed her eyes. "For now."

His shoulders relaxed. "Good. I'm starving. Let's order breakfast."

ANG LOOKED across the table at the empty plates piled up. "God, I can't believe we ate all that. I totally fat-guyed it."

Hoyt raised a brow.

Ang shrugged. "One of my college roommates used to say that whenever we pigged out."

"Well, we did work up quite an appetite," he said, grinning at the memory. He'd fully intended to make a hasty departure as soon as he woke up. He'd never expected to feel so . . . comfortable.

"Yes, we did. And now we have to get to work," she said, standing up and stretching.

Hoyt had a sudden desire to reach inside the kimono . . . *No,* he shook his head. Last night was supposed to take care of that. "I'm going back to my room and take a shower," he muttered. *A cold one. Again.*

As he shut the door, Ang chuckled to herself at his abrupt exit, feeling more than a little satisfied with her ability to rattle a man like John Hoyt.

So he'd been a Navy SEAL. That certainly explained Ward's confidence in him. He'd been the best of the best. *And he certainly had been last night,* she thought with a sigh. Way better than her late night fantasy.

She felt good. Damned good. Her body was relaxed. Satisfied. Her mind focused.

Maybe good sex was the key to solving the case. And John Hoyt had not disappointed. She laughed and smiled. Then shook her head as she headed for the shower. Time to get into work mode.

It was Saturday, but they couldn't exactly take the day off. Not on a case like this. Their plan for the day was to surveil the senator. Hoyt had parked a half block down from his house. It was ten a.m. and they'd been parked for an hour and a half.

Ang was already antsy. She fidgeted in her seat. This was definitely the worst part of the job for her. Hoyt, however, seemed to be content to quietly and intensely focus on the senator's house. He barely moved. She wanted to poke him just to get a reaction. And she knew from the night before just how reactive he could be. The thought made her smile.

"What?" he asked, turning towards her.

"Nothing." She fought back a laugh

He raised a brow but didn't press her, just turned his attention back to the house.

Ten minutes later, the garage door went up. *Finally,* she thought.

Hoyt started the car and followed the senator's dark blue Mercedes, keeping a few car lengths back. When the car pulled into a movie theatre parking lot, Hoyt kept going, circled the block, then parked a few spots down from the senator's car.

"Now what?" Ang asked.

"We wait."

"For two hours?"

Hoyt shrugged. "Welcome to the world of surveillance."

"You do this a lot in the military?"

"Some."

Ang sighed.

"We'll be here a while. You want to go grab us some coffee and food?"

Ang exited the car without a second glance.

After the movie, they followed as the senator dropped his wife off at home, then went to the local golf club, where he emerged an hour later looking slightly drunk.

"Too bad the cops in this town won't do anything if he gets pulled over," Ang muttered.

They followed him home and watched the lights come on in the house.

"I think he's in for the night," Hoyt said. "We'll let Sanderson's guy take over from here."

Ang rolled her neck and stretched as he made the call to Sanderson, stiff from being in the car all day.

"Well, that was fun," she said once they were back in the hotel. Hoyt just smiled as he walked her to her room.

Ang yawned. "I need a shower. Then bed."

Hoyt leaned forward, angling his face towards hers, and kissed her deeply.

He slowly pulled back and Ang looked up at him, blinking softly.

"Get some sleep," he said. "I'll see you in the morning." He headed back down the hall, trying to not picture her naked in the shower.

HOYT GRABBED his phone and grinned when he saw Lash Brogan's name on the caller ID later that night. "How's the celebrity life?" he asked as he answered.

"Boring. How's the FBI life?" the familiar Irish brogue asked.

"Your life has never been boring."

"I hear yours isn't exactly boring either since you left the body-guard business."

"What's that supposed to mean?" Hoyt asked.

"Lauren and I had dinner with Ward last weekend. He said you've got yourself a hot little partner."

Hoyt groaned. "Ang's my partner, nothing more."

"Yeah, I can tell by the defensive tone in your voice."

"Ward has a big fucking mouth."

Lash laughed. "It's good to know there's someone in the world who can get under your skin. She must really be something."

And she was. That was the truth. She always spoke what she felt and wasn't afraid to put him in his place. They had different ways of going about an investigation. He was more of a go out on the street and talk to people person while she wanted to know the background first before jumping in. Hoyt rubbed his forehead, forced his thoughts back to the present. "Was there a reason you called?"

"Nope. Just wanted to harass you."

"How's Rafe doing?" Hoyt asked, hoping to re-direct the conversation.

"Pretty damned good. You trained him well."

"Good. We'll have to all catch up when this case is over."

"Sounds good. We'll have you and your new lady friend over for dinner."

"Fuck you."

"Well, I'm glad we had this talk," Lash said. "Give me a ring when you've got some time off."

Hoyt hung up. He did not want to think about Ang. Sex was one thing, and it was damned good with her, no question. But relation-ships, that was a whole new territory for him. One he wasn't comfort-able with. But the thought of not having her in his life, well damn, that just wasn't acceptable.

7

The next morning, Ang and Hoyt sat in the small conference room at the RA, waiting on Ward to answer the phone.

They listened to the ringing on the speaker phone.

"What's the latest?" Ward asked, finally answering.

"Not much, sir," Hoyt answered, frowning.

Sanderson entered the room, looking harried as usual. "Sorry I'm late. Had a call with the Cheyenne office."

"Anything new on Chief Delaney?" Hoyt asked him.

Sanderson shook his head.

"Nothing?" Ang asked.

Hoyt looked over his own notes on Chief Delaney and shook his head. "I can't find anything either."

There hadn't been any discrepancies in his financials. The man was being careful. But he was just delaying the inevitable. Hoyt would find a reason to nail the son of a bitch.

After they nailed Senator Westmoreland.

Hoyt clenched his jaw as he stood and paced around the conference room.

"Any progress with the senator or his aide?" Ward asked.

"Nothing worth mentioning, unfortunately," Hoyt said. "Not enough for a search warrant."

"Keep at it. We knew this one wasn't going to be easy," Ward said.

"Yes, sir," Hoyt answered as he hung up the phone. He ran a hand down his face, trying to not let his frustration show. "What's on the agenda for today?" he asked Sanderson.

"I need to get a handle on what's going on with these fires."

"The arsons?" Ang asked. She'd read about them in the paper.

"Yeah, there's too many similarities. What are the chances of three prostitutes dying in random fires in two months?" Sanderson asked. "I don't like it."

"Want us to help you look into them?" Hoyt asked.

"I know it's not your priority, but I could use another set of eyes, or two, on this."

Hoyt looked at Ang. She nodded. "Sure. Give us what you've got," Hoyt said.

He quickly compared the coroners reports from all the cases that involved fires and dead prostitutes. All three of the women had been strangled. Due to the state of the bodies, the coroner couldn't definitively prove it, but had made notes about possible sexual assault. There were too many similarities to ignore. Someone was killing prostitutes and covering it up. Could this be related to what they were already investigating?

Damn. If all the cases he worked were this complicated, his life would never be boring. Especially if it was Ang he was working them with.

"I'll be right back," Ang said. "Too much coffee," she muttered, leaving the room.

"How's your network of informants?" Hoyt asked Sanderson as soon as the door shut behind her.

"Solid," he answered. "There a reason you're asking me about this while you're partner's not here?"

Hoyt was impressed with the other agent's perception, but he didn't feel like justifying himself. "My only priority is to solve this case using whatever means necessary to get the job done," he said.

Sanderson shrugged. "Fair enough. There's a couple guys that might be helpful to you. I'll text you their info."

"Thanks. I appreciate it."

Sanderson nodded curtly. "Anything else?"

"How about another car."

Sanderson gave him a searching look. It made sense for the visiting agents to have two vehicles, but he didn't like the look in Hoyt's eyes. The man was up to something.

"I don't have time to bullshit around, so I'm going to continue putting my trust in you and Agent Nobles. But so help me God, if you do anything to fuck up this case, I will have your ass." He paused. "Although, I have a feeling I'd need to get in line behind Agent Nobles."

Hoyt gave him an easy smile. "My only goal is to end this case and ensure everyone goes home safely."

Sanderson gave him a brief nod and handed over a set of car keys.

Hoyt studied the man in front of him. Despite the other agent's current appearance, Hoyt recognized the mannerisms. The guy had spent time in the military. And not just a basic Army unit. He narrowed his eyes. "Delta?" he guessed.

Sanderson blinked, then gave him a slow grin. "You're good, Hoyt, I'll give you that. What were you?"

"SEAL."

"Figures," Sanderson said. "Fuckin' Navy."

Hoyt grinned. "Maybe we can compare war stories once this is over."

"Deal," Sanderson answered. "I'll buy the first round."

Ang came back into the room and looked from one of them to the other. "What did I miss?"

Hoyt held up the keys. "I scored us a second car."

WHEN THEY GOT BACK to the hotel, Ang went to her room before dinner and Hoyt went to his. He used the opportunity to check his phone. As promised, Sanderson had sent him four names of informants he'd used and brief bios of the men. He'd have to go over them in more detail later, but one stood out as a definite possibility.

Paul Ronson.

The guy was former military, untreated PTSD. He had a wife and two kids who'd moved away recently. There was still a nice house in the suburbs in his name, but the guy was basically living on the streets. Definitely a guy worth following up on.

ANG SIGHED as she kicked off her shoes back in her hotel room. They hadn't made much progress today. It was frustrating and she was exhausted. She was meeting Hoyt in an hour for dinner and hopefully some after dinner activities later. That brought a smile to her face.

Her phone beeped and she continued smiling when she saw her dad's number.

"Hi, Dad."

"Hi sweetie. How's the case going?"

She sighed. "Slow."

"What's Special Agent John Hoyt like?" her father asked.

Impressive, she thought but didn't say. "Capable. Good instincts," she said instead. No need to ask how her father knew who her partner was. The man might be retired, but he still had his ways of finding things out.

Ang was still amazed Ward had hand-picked her partner without asking for her input. She was also amazed at how she'd let Hoyt under her skin. And into her bed. Not that she was going to say any of that to her dad.

"Why didn't you tell me Agent Hoyt's background before I left?" she asked.

"Does it matter?"

"He was a bodyguard for one of the world's biggest celebrities," she nearly shouted.

"And?" her dad asked calmly.

"And . . ." her voice trailed off. "It just seems like something I should have known."

"Why? It's not relevant to the case."

Damn, her dad could irritate the hell out of her. But he did have a valid point. And she sounded like an angry toddler. "You're right," she admitted. "It just surprised me."

"He's a good man from what I hear. And I have every confidence that the two of you will get the job done. Together."

Damned if he didn't sound just like her boss. And what could she say to that?

"Yes, dad," she finally said.

"Be careful," her father said after a long pause.

"What do you mean?" He always could read her too well, even over the phone.

"I mean getting involved with someone you work with."

"Dad, we're not involved." *Not yet, anyway, but very possibly headed in that direction. No. It was just sex. Not a relationship,* she tried to tell herself.

"Well, you could do a hell of a lot worse, I suppose. He knows lots of famous people. He'd certainly make an interesting son-in-law."

"Dad!"

"Love you honey, just be careful. Of your career and your heart."

Damn, but her Dad could read her voice too well. "Love you, too," she said as she hung up.

She sighed. It was all she'd ever wanted. To follow in the family tradition. While other girls had played nonstop Barbie's and dress-up, wearing pink glittery ribbons in their hair, she'd been playing cops and robbers with the boys down the street in mud-streaked jeans.

Special Agent John Hoyt made her want to be a woman. A girly girl woman. For the first time in her life, she wanted to be pretty. Feminine. Not just one of the guys.

She wanted to wear sexy underwear and be seduced with roses and champagne.

She wanted romance.

She wanted him.

And she was obviously out of her damned mind. She never should have slept with him.

The conversation with her father had Ang wondering about Hoyt's past life as a bodyguard. And dammit, the thought of him being around all kinds of beautiful movie stars caused a surge of jealousy she had no right to feel.

Had he slept with anyone famous? He seemed more like the strong, silent type and she was sure he took his job too seriously to get distracted. Of course, he'd allowed her to distract him from his current job, so who knew?

She needed to take a step back, keep her mind from wandering any farther down this path. Yes, they had slept together. They were two single adults who were attracted to each other. It didn't have to interfere with the case. Or complicate her life.

She had to get off this train of thought right now before it derailed not just this case, but her entire career. Focus was what she needed, not a distraction. No matter how nice of an ass the distraction had.

Her stomach growled, reminding her it was time to meet the distraction with a nice ass for dinner.

TWO HOURS LATER, she lay naked next to Hoyt in her bed. He was sound asleep and her own eyes slowly drifted shut. Her body was totally relaxed, all her needs met.

Maybe her worries were for nothing. Maybe they could be partners and lovers.

8

"Where are you going?" Ang asked, the following night. They'd just finished making love and now Hoyt was out of bed and getting dressed again.

"Just out for a bit."

Ang gave him a hard look. "It's eleven at night."

Hoyt shrugged. He wasn't used to anyone being able to read him as well as she did.

She cocked her head.

He pulled his shirt over his head. "Sanderson gave me a list of informants he's used. A couple look like they might be useful. I'm going to meet with one of them."

"And when, exactly, where you planning on telling me about this?"

Hoyt sighed. He also wasn't used to having a partner. Sure, he'd been part of a team in the military and as a bodyguard, but he'd always had the freedom to make his own decisions in the field. "If I found out anything useful."

"Dammit, Hoyt. When are you ever going to get it through your thick skull that we're a team? Did you ever consider the fact that I could help? That maybe I would be the better one to meet with the informant? Or that you might need backup?"

He put his hands on his hips, clearly frustrated. She was right, of course. He should have told her about the meeting. But if the needs of the case or the need to keep her safe warranted it, he would do it again. In a heartbeat. But there was no easy way to explain it to her that wouldn't piss her off.

"Look, I get that you're used to calling the shots," she said. "But give me some credit. I'm a good agent. This isn't your case. It's *our* case."

He smiled and damned if it didn't ease her anger. "You're right," he said.

Her mouth opened but she didn't know what to say.

"And you're cute when you're flustered." He finished getting dressed, slipped on his holster and gun as she glared up at him from the bed. "Well, are you coming or what?" he asked.

"Asshole," she muttered as she hurriedly jumped out of bed and got dressed.

He turned to her as he drove through the dark city streets. "This guy is a loner. He's unstable and an alcoholic. He's also an insomniac and likes to wander the city at night. He looks homeless, so no one pays attention to him. He may have seen or heard something during our fires or have a lead on the drug connection."

Ang looked out the window as they turned down a street in a run-down part of the city. "*Is* this guy homeless?"

Hoyt shook his head. "No. He has a home, he just doesn't live there much."

He pulled into a liquor store parking lot. "Be right back," he said.

Ang locked the door as soon as he left the car. It might be Casper, WY, but it wasn't exactly a nice-looking part of town.

She watched him stalk back towards the car a few minutes later. With his black shirt and jeans and the dangerous look on his face, he looked like he fit into the shady neighborhood just fine.

He opened the door and handed her a bottle wrapped in a paper bag. "A little bribe won't hurt."

He started the car again. "I'm meeting him at a park down the street. When we stop, move into the driver's seat and I'll message you if I need you."

She nodded.

Twenty minutes later, she was still sitting in the car alone. She sat up straighter as she saw two figures emerge from the dark shadows. They had their arms around each other's shoulders as they stumbled from the trees. *Good thing she was here to drive back to the hotel*, she thought.

She kept watch as they separated, one of them weaving away from the park. The other man stood, then turned and walked towards her, his gait steady.

She let out a breath as Hoyt opened the passenger door.

"How'd it go?" she asked.

"He didn't see anything, but might know someone who did."

She studied him. "You're not drunk."

He laughed. "Not even close. I just let him think I was."

ACROSS TOWN, two men sat in a back booth in a dark bar.

"So, we agree there's nothing suspicious going on?" Ed asked, taking a drink of his beer.

Police Chief Delaney hadn't been surprised when Ed wanted to meet. The timing was too coincidental. He was well aware who they were both protecting, not that either of them would mention the man's name out loud. But covering up murder with arson? This was going way beyond what the senator had originally proposed. This was outright murder.

He looked across the table. He knew Ed. They'd both been so full of hope and ideals when they were young. They'd grown up together, determined to make a difference. To protect the citizens of Casper, he as a cop and Ed fighting fires. So what the hell had happened to them? He took a long drink of his whiskey.

They barely spoke to each other now outside of work. Other than an occasional meeting at a back booth in the bar.

But he was in too far to get out now. They both were. He needed to shake off his dark mood. He thought of the balance in his bank account and smiled. "Nothing suspicious that I can see," he said.

"Good," Ed said. He'd been hoping for reassurance that the police chief was still on board. He'd had his doubts. But he was not going to give up his new position and the senator needed reassurances. Delaney had always been a weak link, clinging to a warped sense of right and wrong. But ultimately, greed won out, as it usually did. "I heard the visiting FBI agents paid you a visit," he said draining the last of his beer.

"Don't worry, I didn't give them anything. Just kicked the mother-fuckers out of my office."

"Good," Ed said again. "This will all blow over soon," he said, forcing himself to believe the words.

9

Hoyt had never made love with a woman he cared about. Until Ang. What he couldn't figure out was why it was different with her? It was getting harder and harder for him to spend the night apart from her. And he was definitely not comfortable with that fact.

He'd perfected the art of sex without emotional connection long ago and had no intention of changing his ways. And his jobs hadn't exactly been conducive to having a successful relationship. He'd always been able to walk away from the few women he'd had affairs with.

But this woman was different. It wasn't just that she was good in bed, and she *was* spectacular in that area. She'd somehow gotten into his head, under his skin, into his cells.

Working with her wasn't enough. Sleeping with her wasn't enough. He wanted every part of her. She made him care, brought out uncomfortable feelings he didn't want, yet somehow needed. And damned if he knew what to do with them.

But the case would end. That was reality.

And in the end, he'd be an asshole like he always was. There was no reason to pretend it could be anything different. There were no happily-ever-afters for guys like him.

He didn't need saving. And yet, he couldn't shake the feeling that he somehow *needed* this woman. That he would never be the same without her in his life.

He was so fucked.

Getting drunk alone in his hotel room was not the answer. At least that's what he tried to tell himself as he refilled his plastic cup with tequila. Again.

He picked up his cell phone. Lash answered after two rings.

"How the fuck are you?" Lash asked in his Irish brogue that was just pronounced enough to suggest he'd had more than one whiskey.

"Hanging in there. How are you?"

Lash laughed. "Liar. And I'm good. Lauren's sleeping. I'm looking at scripts Andy sent over. Guy's a damned slave driver."

Hoyt knew Lash's agent well. "Only when you need it."

Lash grunted, then paused. "True. But enough about me. How are you really? How's the case going?"

"The case is going. It's messy, but we're making progress."

"That's good. And how's your hot little partner?"

Hoyt couldn't find the words, took another drink. "Ang is . . . ah, fuck me."

Lash laughed again. "You're drunk. And knowing how rare that is for you, I'm guessing you finally met your match." He paused. "What the fuck are you drinking anyway?"

"Tequila."

Lash groaned. "Didn't I teach you anything?"

"Never developed a taste for whiskey."

"You're going to feel like shit in the morning," Lash said.

"I know."

"So, your partner, she got to you," Lash prompted.

Hoyt rubbed his forehead. "How did you know Lauren was it for you?" Hoyt asked. He'd been there, he'd seen it unfold. It had been the one bright spot in the movie that had seemed to be cursed. But he wanted to know why she'd been the one.

"Ah, man. *I'm* not drunk enough for this conversation."

Hoyt heard the sounds of ice clinking in a glass. Then a liquid being poured.

"Hold on," Lash said, drinking. He finished his drink, groaned. "Ah, okay then. I think I'm catching up with you."

Hoyt took another drink. Waited.

Lash finally spoke, "You know how losing Justine gutted me. It almost killed me. It may have if you hadn't been there to pull me back. I never expected to fall in love with another woman. Ever. And I fought it with Lauren, but that day she was kidnapped, I knew I would gladly die to keep her safe. I couldn't imagine not having her in my life. And how fucking stupid I was to deny it." The raw emotion in his voice was all too clear.

"I know the feeling. I can't stand thinking about Ang in danger."

"Yeah, you're pretty much fucked, my friend," Lash slurred.

Hoyt finally laughed. "I'll figure it out. Thanks for listening."

"Anytime."

ANG STUDIED Hoyt over breakfast the next morning. He wasn't eating, just pushing his food around on his plate and drinking massive quantities of coffee. When he did look at her, she could see his eyes were bloodshot. In short, he looked like shit.

"Rough night?" she asked softly.

He grunted, drank more coffee.

Ang fought down her annoyance. Was it really her business if he'd gone out and partied the night before?

It was if it affected his ability to do his job. And it wasn't like John Hoyt was the go out and party type. So what the hell had happened? Had something happened in his personal life? She couldn't deny that his not confiding in her hurt. It shouldn't. They were sleeping together, not in a committed relationship. There was a big difference.

But they *were* partners, dammit.

He finally pushed his nearly full plate aside, drained his coffee cup. "Ready to go?" he asked, his voice rough.

"Sure," she answered.

Hoyt led the way outside, squinted as the bright sunlight stabbed through his brain. He hated not being at a hundred percent, knew it was his own damned fault. He also knew Ang had questions, but he damned sure didn't want to tell her that he'd gotten drunk off his ass brooding over his feelings for her.

There was a part of him that thought that was exactly what he should do, but he ignored it.

He didn't deserve someone like her. At least, that's what he told himself. He was too damaged, too stuck in his ways, too . . . whatever the fuck he needed to tell himself to make the words true.

But for the first time in his life, he wanted to be better than that. Wanted to be worthy of this woman next to him.

He needed to get a grip before he put the case and his entire career in jeopardy.

So he ignored her as she followed him to the car.

Neither spoke on the way to the RA.

Agent Sanderson looked from one of them to the other when they entered the conference room. His jaw clenched and he scowled, shook his head, then glared at them both. "Look, I don't care whatever the hell is or isn't going on between the two of you, but you could cut the tension between the two of you with a knife right now. I need you to leave it outside. We've got bigger problems to worry about."

Ang ducked her head, her face flushed in embarrassment. She knew better than to let personal issues show at work. It was a rookie mistake.

Hoyt swallowed hard. "What happened?" he asked.

"There's been another fire. And another body. At an apartment building downtown."

"Shit," Hoyt muttered.

"I was waiting for you guys to get a look at the scene."

"Let's go," Hoyt said.

No one spoke on the drive across town.

They flashed their badges and made their way through the crowd of firefighters and police officers. The fire was out, but smoke still drifted from the wreckage. And the smell. *God, the smell,* Ang thought as they made their way into the apartment building.

Hoyt didn't like seeing Ang's pale face. She was holding it together, but barely.

When she quickly excused herself and disappeared around the side of the building, he followed.

She was bent over, hands on her knees, purging her breakfast into the grass.

He put a hand on her back, rubbed gently up and down.

She stood, wiped her mouth. "Sorry," she said. The cool October air felt good against her clammy forehead.

"Don't apologize." He swallowed hard, fighting down his own bile.

She watched him closely. "How are you doing?"

"Not the best day to come to work with a hangover," he admitted. He swallowed hard again, cleared his throat.

"About that," she said. "What the hell did you do last night anyway?"

"Stayed in my room."

Her eyes narrowed.

"And drank tequila and talked to Lash for a while."

Ang had no idea what to say to that.

"He gave me some advice."

"Oh," she said.

He stepped closer. "See, I can't quite figure out what to do about my feelings for you."

Ang wasn't sure what to think about Hoyt discussing whatever the hell it was between the two of them with one of the biggest movie stars in the entire world. "Did it help?" she asked.

"The drinking or the conversation?"

"Either," she said with a small grin.

Hoyt smiled back. "They both made me realize that I'm crazy about you and have no idea what to do about it."

His honesty touched her. "Well, we'll just have to face the crazy together."

He took her hand. "We better get back before Sanderson sends out a search party."

They made their way around the building. He gave her hand a squeeze before releasing it.

"Feeling better?" Sanderson asked when they were back inside the apartment.

"Definitely," Ang answered.

———

10

B ack at the RA, they gathered in Sanderson's office to go over their notes from the scene.

"Has to be arson. No matter what the fire department says. We can't trust what they say. Not now," Sanderson said.

Hours later, they still didn't have an easy answer. Sanderson's stomach growled and he looked at the clock. Seven p.m. "Let's get out of here," he suggested.

Hoyt stood, stretched out his back. "Where do you have in mind?"

"There's a small out-of-the way bar not far from here. We can get some food and drinks, brainstorm for a bit."

"Sounds good," Hoyt said as Ang nodded.

They followed Sanderson across town for about ten minutes.

"Looks like a dump," Ang said, as Hoyt parked in front of a run-down looking bar and grill. Hoyt shrugged and got out of the car.

Inside, the place was dark, but clean and mostly full. Sanderson led the way to a table in the back.

Once they had their drinks, Sanderson took a long drink of his beer. "I keep thinking there has to be a connection between the senator's case and the fires."

"You think somehow the senator or the police chief are covering them up?" Ang asked.

"I don't know. The whole thing is so convoluted."

"We know we've got a corrupt police chief. We know the senator is dirty. If the fires are being covered up, the fire chief has to know," Hoyt said.

"Too much of a coincidence for all three to be dirty. It has to tie together somehow," Sanderson said.

"Jesus, it's like a trifecta of evil," Hoyt said.

"Any drugs found at the fires?" Ang asked.

Sanderson shook his head.

"The fire chief and the senator, what's the connection?" Ang asked.

Hoyt shrugged. "How is the senator connected to the fires? It doesn't add up."

"He was accused of sexual assault when he was in college," Sanderson said.

"That was a long time ago," Ang said.

"But we can't ignore the fact that these women were sexually assaulted too. Doesn't matter that they were prostitutes," Hoyt said.

"It's a pretty thin connection," Sanderson said. "The senator doesn't have any arrest records, nothing connecting him to prostitutes."

Their burgers and fries arrived and they all dug in.

Ang sighed. "Damn, this is good."

"Place may not look like much, but the food is outstanding," Sanderson said.

"Let's dig deep into these guys' backgrounds. See if we can find any common denominator," Sanderson said when they'd finished eating.

"I'll keep working the informant," Hoyt said.

"I'm going to order another round so we can all take a little while to shut down and relax," Ang said.

Another round turned into two. Ang had tuned both men out as they debated the pros and cons of being a Navy SEAL or an Army

Delta Operator. "Look, let's agree that you're both badasses and call it a night."

Sanderson laughed. He finished his beer and looked hard at Hoyt. "Looks like you'll have your hands full."

Ang glared at them both. Then she finished her beer. "Lightweights," she muttered, leading the way to their cars.

"Lightweights?" Hoyt asked as he drove them back to the hotel.

Ang shrugged and sighed. "A few beers and all you guys can do is compare war stories and dick sizes."

Hoyt laughed. "Let's get back to the room and I'll prove to you how superior the SEALs are."

Ang turned and smiled. "I accept your challenge."

WHILE IT WAS nice having a boss that was hands on and wanted to be involved in every step of the case, Hoyt couldn't help but wonder if the SAC's decision to come to Casper now had anything to do with the lack of progress he and Ang had made so far. Or the latest dead body that was looking more and more like a serial killer.

Hoyt had offered to pick Ward up from the airport so Ang could sleep in if she wanted. But now, seeing the stern, scowling face of his boss waiting at the curb of the small airport, he quickly regretted his decision.

He took a deep breath and parked the car.

"Sir," Hoyt said, as he opened the trunk for Ward's suitcase.

Ward just grunted as he put his bag inside, then made his way to the passenger seat.

Hoyt clenched his jaw and got back in the car, headed towards the airport exit.

"Goddamn, I hate flying." Ward finally spoke. "Makes me wish like hell I hadn't given up smoking."

Hoyt chuckled. "Welcome to Casper, sir."

Ward ran a hand down his face. "Agent Nobles back at the hotel?"

Hoyt nodded. "Figured I'd let her sleep in." He didn't add that he was part of the reason she was tired. When they'd gotten back to the hotel after dinner and drinks with Sanderson he'd apologized again for being an ass at the fire scene and miracle of miracles, she'd forgiven him. They'd finally exhausted each other just after two in the morning. He fought down the smile the memory evoked. The last thing he needed was Ward knowing about the two of them.

AN HOUR AND A HALF LATER, they were all gathered in Ward's suite.

Hoyt had just started giving the latest update when Ward looked from him to Ang and laughed.

Hoyt looked up from his notes. "I'm not telling jokes here, Ward." He paused. "Sir," he added. Just because he knew the man didn't change the fact that he was now his boss.

"It's about damn time," Ward said with a grin.

"Excuse me?" Hoyt asked.

"The two of you. I think it's great. Seriously."

Ang's face reddened slightly. She should have known Ward would see what was going on between her and Hoyt, he was way too damned good at reading people. "I don't think that's relevant to the case," she managed to say.

"It isn't." Ward turned his gaze back to Hoyt. "As long as it doesn't interfere with the job."

"It won't. Now can I continue with my presentation?"

"By all means." Ward gestured for him to continue.

Hoyt finished getting Ward up to speed on their progress, or lack of it, on the case. He finished with his notes on the fires. "I think they could be related, I'm just not sure how."

Ward rubbed his forehead. "There's definitely something here with the fires. Just keep in mind, the senator is our first priority. We can't get discouraged. Not now. Cases like this have a nasty way of getting worse before they get better. It's been a long fucking day, and it's getting late, you guys want to get dinner and some drinks?"

"I think Ang and I should turn in early tonight," Hoyt said.

Ang felt a sudden rush of warm wetness between her thighs

thinking of John Hoyt and a bed. She crossed her legs, couldn't bring herself to look at her boss.

Hoyt gave her a look that said he knew exactly where her mind had gone. He winked at her.

Ward cleared his throat and stood. He glanced at his watch. "Enjoy your *sleep*. I'll see you two at breakfast."

AT SEVEN THE NEXT MORNING, Ward poured himself a to-go cup of coffee and grabbed a banana, ignoring the rest of the continental breakfast at the hotel. He saw Agents Hoyt and Nobles at a table in the corner of the room.

They both started to stand as he approached. He motioned them to remain seated.

"Join us," Hoyt said.

Ward shook his head. "Think I'll head over to the RA. Meet Agent Sanderson in person."

Hoyt handed him the car keys. "We'll take the other car."

"We can go with you," Ang said.

"No. Stay and enjoy your breakfast. It's about time I got to know the new head of our Casper office. I'll see you guys over there in a little while."

"Think we should warn Sanderson he's coming?" Ang asked after their boss had left.

"Nah, I think he can handle it," Hoyt answered with a grin.

AGENT SANDERSON HAD JUST FINISHED his take-out fast food breakfast sandwich when Special Agent Ward Calhoun walked into his office.

"Sir," Sanderson said, wiping his greasy hands on a napkin and standing up straight. He'd never met the Denver SAC, but recognized him from the numerous pictures and articles he's seen. He probably should have at least gotten a haircut, he thought, but it wasn't like he'd had the time since his abrupt promotion. And after spending years in the military with a buzz cut, he liked the small act of rebellion.

Ward fought back a smile at the other agent's discomfort. "Relax, agent. I know your background and I don't give a shit if you look like you should be on a beach in California instead of an FBI office. I only care about how well you can do the job."

"Sir," Sanderson said, not knowing what else to say.

"And from what I've heard, you've been doing a damned good job, considering the circumstances."

"Thank you."

"Now, let's get some coffee and go over those files."

Sanderson relaxed slightly and led the way to the coffee machine.

"You getting along okay with my agents?" Ward asked.

Sanderson sensed a trick question. "Probably better than most."

"Hoyt's good. He's damned good, but I know he likes to do things on his own. I appreciate your calm levelheadeness. You can help keep him in line."

Sanderson laughed. "I don't know about that, sir.

Ward took a sip of coffee. "Explain."

"I'm not going to get into the man's business, but I think he'd color outside every line there is to keep his partner out of harm's way."

Ward laughed and shook his head.

"You're not surprised?" Sanderson asked.

"No. I saw this coming from day one."

Sanderson wasn't sure what to say to that. "In all seriousness, I don't think there's anyone better than those two to figure this thing out."

"And you," Ward added. "You've done good work here. I'm impressed."

"Thank you, sir. I just wish we were closer to getting this mess sorted out."

"It'll come. Now, let's see what you've got."

Sanderson pulled out several folders, then clicked on the computer.

. . .

HOYT COULDN'T CONCENTRATE. He'd headed back up to his room after breakfast. But his room had felt stifling, so he had moved down to the hotel lobby. He sat with a cup of coffee and tried to read Ward's report on the senator's financials for the fifth time. Images of Ang's naked body kept popping into his head. He closed the file and rubbed his eyes. Sleeping with her had only made things worse. He had to find a way to get past this before he lost his job or drove himself crazy. He'd never had a woman get inside his head like this. He needed to fucking get a grip. She was just a woman.

A smart, drop dead gorgeous woman, yes, but still just a woman.

He had almost managed to convince himself that he could handle working the case and the developing relationship with Ang. Then she walked down the hall towards him and his heart and stomach contracted. *Son of a bitch*, he thought. And knew he'd give his life to have her again.

But he had no fucking idea how to put it into words. He didn't do relationships. He was in way over his head.

She cocked her head to the side, studying him.

Hoyt forced a neutral expression on his face. "Let's go."

He didn't speak to her during the entire drive to the RA and he almost wished Ward had waited to catch a ride with them. He couldn't help but flinch as she slammed the car door when she got out.

What the hell had he done wrong now?

Women.

WARD COULD FEEL the tension between his agents. They were obviously sleeping together. But was it turning into more? He knew it wasn't his place to say anything. Whatever was or wasn't happening between the two of them, he knew they were both trying their damnedest to solve the case.

And it wasn't like he had any profound advice to offer either of them. He was a workaholic with one divorce under his belt. But the connection between the two agents was something that couldn't be ignored for long. They'd have to deal with it one way or another.

He shook his head, focused on the present.

It had been another long day. They'd gotten back to the hotel and headed straight for the bar. Ang was across the room on the phone with her dad, walking back and forth across the room, sipping her wine. Maybe her old man would have some insights.

Hoyt and Ward sat at the bar with frosty mugs of beer.

"Have you talked to that infamous brother-in-law of yours lately?" Hoyt asked.

Ward gave a rare grin and shook his head. "I have. I still have a hard time believing my little sister actually married the guy."

"As long as they're happy."

Ward's face grew serious. "They are."

"I know. I'm glad."

"Yeah, they both deserve it. I had my reservations about the guy, but Lash is completely devoted to Lauren."

"He's a good man," Hoyt said.

"Yes, he is."

Ward realized he and Hoyt might have more in common than he'd originally thought. But Hoyt was smart enough not to get married. Ward had made that mistake once and that had been enough. But sometimes, late at night, he felt a longing for someone to hold, someone to love. Maybe he was just getting old. He took a long drink.

He watched Hoyt watch Ang, said, "I don't want you to end up like me."

"What do you mean?"

Ward nodded at Ang. "I mean her. You and her."

Hoyt smiled, then sighed. "She's my partner, Ward."

Ward took a drink and shrugged. "Looks like it could be much more than a simple affair."

Hoyt finished his own drink, wishing the alcohol hadn't started to dissolve his self-control. It made it too damned easy to talk, too easy to let the words and emotions flow. This was why he avoided getting drunk. "I don't think I'm capable of more," he said, honestly.

"Time will tell," Ward answered.

"Yeah. And we have more important things to think about here."

Ward put up his hands. "Fair enough."

But Hoyt couldn't stop his mind from drifting to Ang. "Doesn't the bureau frown on relationships between agents?" he asked.

"It does add a whole level of complicated, but it's not unheard of," Ward answered.

Hoyt sighed, ran a hand down his face. Complicated was not something he needed.

But then he looked at Ang across the room and wondered if maybe it was *exactly* what he needed.

ANG HUNG up the phone and walked towards the bar where Hoyt and Ward were having what looked like an intense conversation. She wondered what the topic was.

Hoyt barely looked at her as she approached. She wished she didn't care.

"Refill?" Ward asked.

"No, thank you. I'm tired, so I think I'll head up to my room. See you guys in the morning."

She sighed and retreated to the bathroom as soon as she entered her hotel room. She turned on the water, adding a generous amount of her favorite bubble bath. She definitely needed to soak away the day.

Stepping into the warm, fragrant water was heaven. She closed her eyes, leaned her head back and let the warmth seep into her knotted muscles. The soothing scent of lavender surrounded her and she breathed in deeply.

She shouldn't be hurt by Hoyt's behavior. He was just being a man. And they had made zero promises to each other. And she didn't want them.

Did she?

So he'd said he was crazy about her. But what the hell did that even mean?

She ducked her head down under the water.

Sex. No strings. Solve the case. Go home.

She sat back up and wiped the water from her eyes. Sounded simple enough she could almost believe it.

11

Two days later, Hoyt couldn't stand the subtle tension with Ang. He'd stayed late at the RA, sorting through financial records with Ward and Sanderson.

Now, back at the hotel, he went straight to Ang's room. He needed to clear the air with her.

She opened the door and let him in without a word. She had her hair pulled up and was in yoga pants and a long baggy sweatshirt. She made his mouth water.

Ang watched him and laughed. "If I knew yoga pants turned you on that much, I would have broken them out sooner."

Hoyt wasn't used to having someone read him as well as she did. "Sorry," he said.

She raised an eyebrow.

"I'm sorry for staring at your very fine ass." He paused. "And I'm sorry for being an ass."

Ang sighed and all traces of laughter disappeared. "Should we try to go back to just being partners?"

"I don't know if I can," Hoyt admitted. "This is all new territory for me. I know I'm fucking it up. I don't mean to."

"I think we need to spend less time trying to complicate things and just enjoy each other while we solve this case."

"You make it sound so simple," he said.

She shrugged. "Maybe it can be."

Hoyt had his doubts, but he was certainly willing to give it a try. "Okay, how about I go grab us dinner. Then we can work for a couple hours."

"Do you miss working for Lash Brogan?" Ang asked as she settled herself onto the couch later that night after they'd eaten.

Hoyt threw their empty pizza box in the trash.

As a general rule, he didn't like talking about those days. Not that he regretted them, he just didn't like advertising the fact that he'd been a celebrity bodyguard. But for some reason, he didn't mind talking to Ang about it. He actually quite enjoyed it, which was a definite first for him.

"Sometimes," he answered honestly. "I was overpaid for sure. And it was a good gig, except for the taking a bullet part. But it was time to leave. Lash had become a friend."

"Why was that a problem?" she asked.

"It's too hard to keep a distance, to be a good protector, when you start socializing with your protectee."

He paused, thinking how easy it could be to slip into the same situation with Ang. Could they really be partners and lovers?

He watched as she cocked her head, as if she knew exactly what he was thinking. She was way too damned in tune with him.

"You know this is different, right? We're partners. Fifty-fifty. We look out for each other equally. It's not your job to protect me," she said.

He knew she was right, but she sure as hell brought out his protective instincts. But he knew it would piss her off if he said it out loud. So he kept his mouth shut.

She held his gaze for a moment, then her face softened. "Well, since we got that settled, let's finish our work so we can enjoy the rest of our evening."

And that was all the motivation he needed. He forced himself to focus on the task at hand so he could get her naked and in bed.

Later that night, he watched her in the moonlight as she fell asleep.

He'd never done that before, with any woman. Never cared enough to.

He breathed in her subtle scent of lavender, felt her small warm body pressed up against his, and drifted off into a peaceful sleep.

HOYT FINISHED his coffee early the next morning, set the cup aside as he looked over their case notes. After spending the night together in Ang's room, they had ordered room service for breakfast. Being with Ang was almost too easy. They complimented each other in and out of bed. He couldn't begin to explain it, yet alone understand it.

They'd even exchanged keys for their rooms. Not that it was anything like a key to their real places. But it was significant to him.

He shook his head, forced himself to focus on the pictures of the small airport outside of town where they hoped to catch some of the senator's men in the act of smuggling in drugs, thanks to a tip from an anonymous caller.

"This could be the break we need. Intel seems solid," he said as Ang came out of the bathroom, dressed and ready to go.

"So what's the plan?" she asked.

"We go in, take a look around, call in Sanderson and the cops if we find what we're looking for." He downed the last of his coffee.

"Okay." She stood, strapped on her holster and shrugged into her jacket as Hoyt did the same. He marveled at how in sync they were, how they moved as a team. He liked it a hell of a lot.

THE AIRPORT WAS DESERTED, as expected that early in the morning. They'd cleared the main building and all of the hangars when the sound of a car coming down the gravel road carried across the still air.

It was quickly followed by the sound of an airplane approaching.

"Shit," Hoyt muttered, pulling Ang behind one of the buildings.

The small four-seat plane was on final approach now. No way to make it back to their car without breaking cover.

"Let's wait, see who we're dealing with. Could be an innocent pilot," Hoyt said.

Ang nodded as they watched the plane land.

All illusions of innocence disappeared at the sight of the armed men exiting both the plane and the car.

Hoyt frowned as he studied the men. Possibly Columbian and well armed with AR 223 rifles. "Well, I guess that's why we didn't find anything. Drugs must be on the plane," he said.

Two of the men were looking in the windows of their bureau car, parked in front of the FBO. One of them turned and gestured at several of the others.

"Find them. Now," the man yelled, then shot out the tires of their bureau car.

Hoyt's jaw clenched and he checked his gun. They were outnumbered eight to two. Not good odds. Especially with how heavily armed the bad guys were.

THEY WERE OUTNUMBERED AND OUTGUNNED. Their car had been disabled. They were out of options. There was no way out that Ang could see. She imagined how Agent Calhoun would break the news of her death to her father. *"We regret to inform you that your daughter was killed in the line of duty ..."*

Then Hoyt was grabbing her arm and pulling her through a door and into one of the hangars. Before she knew what was going on, he'd picked the lock to the small plane that sat inside of the rusted metal building.

"Get in," he said tersely.

"What?" she asked.

Hoyt just glared at her. "If you want to live, get in the fucking plane right now."

Her partner's commanding voice had her instantly moving. The tiny metal door groaned as she opened it and strapped herself in. Hoyt leaned inside and cranked the engine, then threw open the main hangar door. He ran back, jumped inside the cockpit and slammed the door shut as his hands worked the controls. "Open the side window and shoot anyone you see," he said, easing the plane forward.

Ang glanced around the cockpit at the dirty carpet and upholstery, the cracked leather dash. "Will this rusty piece of shit fly?"

Hoyt shrugged as he eased the plane out of the hanger. "We'll find out."

It didn't take long for the bad guys to figure out what they intended and they all converged on the small plane, firing directly at it. Ang returned fire, taking down two of them with well-placed shots.

Hoyt gunned the engine, swerved onto the runway, and jerked back the yoke. The engine sputtered, the tiny plane bumped up and back down, then slowly, slowly started to climb into the clear blue sky. Ang ducked as she heard a few stray shots hit the aluminum skin of the plane, one cracking the windshield between them.

"Can you really fly this thing?" she asked over the engine noise when they were clear.

Hoyt didn't answer, just concentrated on the instrument gauges and worked the controls. After a few tense, very turbulent minutes, he turned towards her. "Our left fuel tank's leaking and the tail must be shot up pretty bad. I'm having a hard time controlling her." He pointed through the cracked windshield. "I'm going to try to set her down in that field ahead."

Ang swallowed hard and tightened her seatbelt. The plane jerked, lifted and then dropped as Hoyt struggled to keep them in the air and on a steady course. She closed her eyes as the ground got closer and closer. She couldn't help it. She braced herself for the inevitable crash. Was this really how she was going to die?

The plane landed hard, skidded left and right, then the front end dropped into a ravine and her body jerked forward and stopped.

She opened her eyes. They were still alive. *Holy shit.* It took a minute for her to catch her breath. To believe it was real.

Hoyt calmly whipped out his cell phone as he jumped to the ground and came around the other side to help her down out of the battered plane. She heard him give the local cops the GPS coordinates and briefly explain the situation.

She saw the bullet holes and streaks of fuel as she walked around the plane. "Oh my God," she whispered. It was a miracle they were still alive.

Hoyt took her hand and led her a safe distance away. Then they sat down in the middle of the field to wait. "You okay?" he asked.

She managed to nod. "You?"

"Yeah, not my best landing, though," he said with a small smile.

She couldn't help it, maybe it was the start of the adrenaline crash, but she started laughing and couldn't stop for a good long time.

"Jesus," Sanderson said as they gathered back in his office later that afternoon. "You two have managed to stir up more shit in the short time you've been here than anyone I've ever worked with."

"Thanks," Hoyt said with a shrug.

Sanderson glared at him.

"Where's Ward?" Ang asked, looking around.

"Had to head to Cheyenne. They've got a nasty child abduction case going on. He'll be back and forth between here and there."

"Anything at the airport?" Hoyt asked.

Sanderson shook his head. "The bad guys cleared out the bodies, then flew out with the drugs before we could get there. Other than some blood and footprints on the ground, we've got nothing."

"But they know we're onto them. They'll be running scared, more likely to make a mistake," Hoyt said.

"Or to come after you directly if they got a good look at you," Sanderson said.

"I'm not worried about that," Hoyt answered.

Sanderson turned his gaze towards Ang, then back to Hoyt. "Maybe you should be."

Ang shook her head. "Look, the way I see it, we stopped one shipment from hitting the city today. We threw them off their game. They'll be scrambling to figure things out now which could make them more prone to making a mistake. I call that a win."

Hoyt loved that she had his back. "And we've got license plate numbers and we know what guns they carry. We know they're foreign."

Sanderson leaned back. "Okay, so we did get *some* useful information. And you didn't get killed. Good job with that."

Hoyt grinned back. "We do aim to please."

Sanderson rolled his eyes. "Go get some rest. I'll see you guys in the morning."

LATER THAT NIGHT, they ordered room service in Ang's hotel room. Hoyt opened a second bottle of wine after they'd finished the first with dinner, poured them each a generous glass. He raised his glass toward hers. "To survival," he said.

She touched her glass to his and drank deeply. After their crash landing, they'd spent hours with the police and local agents, talked to Sanderson and Ward numerous times, and filled out reams of paperwork. There hadn't been time to process the emotions of what they had been through. Now, after a nice meal and several glasses of wine, she found herself replaying the day's events in her mind, each time more grateful to be alive.

"So I assume today wasn't the first time you've flown a plane," she said.

Hoyt shook his head. "First time I've flown one that small in a long time, though."

"Did you fly in the Navy?"

Hoyt took a long drink. "No. I used to fly Lash Brogan's jet."

Ang nearly inhaled her wine. "Oh, of course, you used to fly movie stars around."

"It wasn't like that."

"What was it like?" she asked, genuinely curious.

"Lash needed someone to fly the jet. He doesn't like a large entourage, so it made sense for me to have my pilot's license." He shrugged. "No big deal."

Ang smiled. "Yeah, no big deal at all." She looked down into her wine, swirled the dark liquid around, watching it coat the glass. "It is impressive. And it sure saved our asses today."

He leaned back in his chair, closed his eyes. "Not a bad skill to have."

She finished her wine, moved to sit on Hoyt's lap. He half-opened his eyes, gave her a wicked grin. "Want to know about my other special skills?"

"I think I've already witnessed a few of them firsthand. But maybe you could take me to the bedroom and refresh my memory."

He stood with her in his arms. "My pleasure."

12

E d looked at the caller ID as his cell phone rang. He hadn't heard from the senator in weeks. He wasn't sure he wanted to know what the other man wanted now. But he couldn't exactly ignore him either. No matter how much he wanted to.

"Senator," he said as he answered.

"I need you to get rid of a body."

No greeting, no lead in. Just those words. *A body?* What the hell had Westmoreland done now? Ed forced himself to wrap his mind around what the senator had just said. "That wasn't our agreement."

"Agreement's changed. You can stage it better than I can. Get rid of the evidence."

"What are you talking about? I fight fires, I can't start one."

"Yes, you can. And you know how to not get caught."

Ed didn't respond. He looked around his new office, at the picture of his wife and him on the beach in Hawaii. But damn, there was a big difference between covering up what the senator had done and starting the fire himself.

"If I go down, you go down. I'm not going to say it again. I need you to do this right now," Westmoreland said, a hard edge to his voice.

There was no mistaking the threat in the senator's words. "Fine. I'll take care of it. Don't let it happen again."

An evil laugh echoed across the line. "It won't happen again. Don't worry."

But they both knew it was a lie. Ed had signed a deal with the devil. He ran a shaky hand down his face. He should have known it wouldn't be that easy.

THE SENATOR WAS, of course, long gone when Ed got to the address the senator and given him. A stern-faced man with a buzz cut waited in the dark shadows. "This way," the man said as Ed approached.

Ed followed the man down an alley and through the boarded up door of a restaurant that had long been closed down. He ignored the rats scurrying away as they entered. The body of a barely dressed young prostitute was lying on the dirty floor, just inside the door, her eyes open and staring, bruises darkening her pale neck. Her left breast was exposed, her panties ripped.

Ed swallowed hard.

"She died in the alley and we drug her in here."

Ed wanted to laugh at the words spoken so matter-of-factly. A United States Senator had raped and strangled a prostitute in a dark alley and he was here to cover it up. Was this really his reality now?

The man with a buzz cut stepped closer. "You going to fix this?"

Ed sighed. "Yes, I'm going to fucking fix it. But you need to get your boss under control before he destroys all of us."

Buzz Cut nodded once and stepped back into the alley.

Ed slowly walked around the dark room, seeing what materials he had to work with.

TYLER COATES, aka Buzz Cut, knew he wasn't a good man. He'd been paid a lot of money for a very long time to look the other way during the years he'd worked for Senator Westmoreland. And he'd enjoyed the freedom that money had given him. There was no doubt about that. He'd grown up dirt poor and still marveled at the balance in his bank account.

It had become too easy to take the money and look the other way.

Sure, there was a small part of him that had wanted to do the right thing, but he'd gotten very good at ignoring it.

But that part of him was growing bigger and he knew why.

His girlfriend was pregnant. The thought produced a surge of warmth in his stomach. And when he thought of his unborn son or daughter, he wanted to be a better man for them. Even if it meant going to jail.

He didn't know how he'd be able to look his child in the eye if he didn't do what was right. What he should have done a long time ago.

Tyler wasn't just a dumbass hired gun. He knew the FBI had been watching the senator for a while. He knew the blond surfer-looking dude was the head of the local office. Then there were the new ones that looked like they might be a couple, the tiny woman and the military-looking guy.

Tyler had served in the Army years ago, one of the few honorable things he'd done in his life. Maybe the shared connection would make the agent go easy on him. It couldn't hurt. And knowing the police chief was unquestionably loyal to the senator, Tyler was shit out of other options.

Now that he knew which one of the agents he was going to contact, he just had to figure out how to do it without drawing the senator's attention.

HOYT HAD FELT like they'd been followed for the past couple of hours. He'd convinced Ang to make a stop at the cafe down the block from the RA, pleading a need for caffeine. "Let's hang out here for a bit, go over our notes," he said as he opened the door for her.

"Sounds good," she said. "It'll be a nice change in scenery."

Hoyt's eyes scanned the room after they'd taken a seat at a table in the corner with their mugs of coffee. His eyes stopped on a muscular blond with a buzz cut standing in line. The guy looked familiar and he searched his memory for where he'd seen him. The man turned and Hoyt got a good look at his face.

He was one of the senator's security guys. Hoyt looked back down at his coffee, sure this was the guy who'd been following them. He knew it in his gut. The question was why?

He forced himself to pay attention to what Ang was saying as he watched the man sit down at a table by himself with a to-go cup of coffee and a newspaper.

Hoyt didn't feel the itchy sensation on the back of his neck that never failed to warn him of danger. The man wasn't a threat. But what did he want?

The man looked up, met Hoyt's eyes, gave a brief nod.

Hoyt took a sip of coffee. "I'll be right back," he said to Ang, heading for the restroom in the back of the building.

Tyler stood, throwing his paper cup in the trash, then turning and bumping into the FBI agent as he walked by.

"Sorry," Tyler muttered, then headed to the front door.

Hoyt continued down the hall, locked the bathroom door behind him, then looked down at the note the other man had slipped him.

10:00 pm Tony's Diner on 52nd

He tucked the note in his pocket and made his way back to the table. This guy could have the information they needed. It was more promising of a lead than anything they'd had lately.

But what was he going to do about it?

HOYT FELT guilty about leaving Ang behind. He'd left her in her hotel room, making up an excuse about needing to check in with Lash about how his new head of security was doing. He justified it by telling himself that it was more inconspicuous for him to go alone. But he had a bad feeling this meet could go sideways and he wasn't about to risk her life unnecessarily.

If he found anything out, he'd let her and Sanderson know.

He tried not to dwell on how easily he could justify his actions.

The diner was within walking distance from their hotel, but he took a longer roundabout way there. The feeling of being watched was there again, but this time his neck was itchy. He felt the comforting weight of his gun in the holster as he approached the diner, glad Ang was safely back at the hotel.

The bell on the door of the diner tinkled as he entered. He looked around. The diner was half-full, but no sign of Buzz Cut. He got a booth that offered a view of the front door, ordered coffee and a slice of apple pie.

Fifteen minutes later, he was still alone with his second cup of coffee and an empty plate.

At least the pie had been good.

He gave it another twenty minutes, then threw some bills down on the table and walked back to the hotel.

He entered Ang's room as quietly as he could, then crawled into bed next to her warm body.

"How was the call?" she asked sleepily.

"Unproductive," he answered, hating himself just a little for lying to her.

"Mmm," she mumbled, snuggling closer to him.

It was a long time before he fell asleep.

TWO BLOCKS from Tony's Diner, Buzz Cut was on his knees in a dark alley. He'd gotten sloppy. He'd been anxious about the meeting and had let his situational awareness slip. Stupid.

Sam Mendez, another of the senator's security guys, shook his head as he pushed the barrel of his gun against Tyler's forehead.

"What the fuck were you doing?" Sam asked.

Tyler looked him in the eye. "Nothing, man. Just headed to get a cup of coffee."

Senator Westmoreland stepped out of the shadows. "Oh? And I suppose it was just a coincidence that FBI Special Agent John Hoyt was alone at a table in the diner down the street? Almost like he was supposed to meet someone there."

Tyler shook his head. "I don't know any Special Agent Hoyt."

"You disappoint me, Tyler." He turned towards Sam. "Make sure the body won't be found for a good long time," the senator said, walking down the alley to where his limo waited at the curb.

"Sam, don't do this," Tyler pleaded. "You *know* me. I didn't do anything wrong."

"But you were about to."

Tyler decided to go with the truth. He had a gun to his head held by a man who had been ordered to kill him. He had nothing else to lose. "I was," he admitted.

Sam blinked in surprise, clearly not expecting that.

"Look, man, you and I both know what the senator's done. And I don't even mean the drugs and other illegal activities. I mean the women."

Sam's jaw clenched.

"You know what I'm talking about."

Sam still didn't respond.

"We can stop him," Tyler pressed on.

"No."

"We can."

"It doesn't matter," Sam said. "I'm not going to jail. No fucking way."

"So you're going to kill me instead?" Tyler asked, thinking of his unborn child.

"I am," Sam said as he fired the silenced gun and Tyler's body toppled over onto the ground of the filthy ally.

13

Two days later, Hoyt and Ang had just sat down to dinner at the hotel restaurant when his phone buzzed. He saw Sanderson's name on his caller ID and immediately answered the phone. "Hoyt."

"It's Sanderson. Got an interesting call from the police department earlier. One of the senator's security guys is missing. Guy's girlfriend filed a missing person's report when he didn't come home a couple nights ago."

"What do you know? Do you think the guy just took off?" Hoyt asked.

"Guy's name is Tyler Coates, big guy, blond buzz cut. Girlfriend's pregnant, said they were doing good. She's pretty broken up."

"Shit." Hoyt's stomach dropped.

"Yeah, seems like a strange coincidence," Sanderson said.

Or maybe not so strange, Hoyt thought. If Westmoreland had somehow found out the guy was going to meet with him . . . Hoyt ran a hand down his face, hoping like hell the guy wasn't dead because of him. *Christ, the guy was going to be a father.* His stomach churned with guilt.

"You still there?" Sanderson asked.

"Yeah, just let us know if you hear anything else."

"Later." Sanderson hung up.

Ang was looking at him with concern. "Something wrong?" she asked.

"One of the senator's security guys is missing. Sanderson's looking into it."

He knew he should tell them both about the meeting he was supposed to have had with the guy. But did it really matter now? The guy was fucking dead. He knew it in his heart.

He wished he could go back and start the whole damned investigation over. There were so many things he'd do differently. Oh, he still would have slept with Ang, there were no regrets there. But he would have been more honest with her, would have shared everything with her. Would have been a true partner.

But it was too late now. He just needed it to be over. He pushed his plate aside.

"Is there something else?" Ang asked.

He shook his head. "No, nothing worth mentioning."

He had tried his best to find out what happened to buzz cut after he'd failed to show for their meeting. His informant hadn't found out a damned thing.

Maybe the guy had chickened out from the meeting and ran. Maybe he was drunk on a beach somewhere. If only Hoyt believed that. No, he was sure the reality was far grimmer. More than likely, the man's body was rotting somewhere in the city.

It ate at him.

IT WAS a week until the next call from the senator. Ed did not want to answer, he felt sick about the possibility of another body. But he had to answer.

"I need you to meet me now. 102 8th Street."

He didn't want to go, but he didn't have a choice. Not now. Not after what they'd both done.

Taking a deep breath, he forced his mind to focus. It didn't matter how he'd gotten into this situation. He had to fix it.

It was a ten minute drive into a not so nice part of town. Ed parked, slowly made his way through the darkness to the address the senator had given him.

It was a run-down warehouse. There was no sign of anyone, but he could hear the faint sounds of a woman crying in the distance. He followed them and had to swallow hard at what he saw.

The senator was squatted down next to a sobbing woman, a muscle-bound man standing silently next to him. Not Buzz Cut. Probably another bodyguard paid extremely well to look the other way.

"I saved her for you," the senator whispered, an evil glint in his eye as he turned towards Ed.

Ed shook his head. "No." The man was clearly not right in the head. He was a United States Senator for God's sake, he wasn't supposed to be a rapist and a killer. What the hell else was he involved in? Ed did not want to know the details. He was already in this too deep.

Westmoreland smiled an evil smile the public never saw. "No one will know. She's just some hooker off the street."

The senator had a crazy look in his eyes. *Jesus, was the guy high?*

Ed looked down at the young woman. Mascara streaks from her tears marred her otherwise perfect face. She was breathing hard, her ample chest moving up and down. Ed felt himself harden despite the situation they were in. Her body was flawless. Young and supple. Unlike his wife at home. He tried to remember the last time they'd even had sex.

His eyes ran over the woman's body again.

Just some hooker off the street.

No one will know.

Something inside him shifted. Ed's doubts started to fade. The danger, the excitement hummed through his veins. No one would know. His hands were already unzipping his fly.

EARLY THE NEXT MORNING, Ed read the newspaper article about the woman's death as he drank his first cup of coffee. He expected to feel remorse at the very least, but felt excitement instead. His dick hardened at the memories and he had to shift in the kitchen chair. *Damn, what a rush it had been.*

He should be alarmed at what was happening to him. He knew he should be. But the excitement was like fighting a gnarly fire. He didn't want to like it, but he did. It was intoxicating. Exhilarating. He wanted to explore these new urges. Unfortunately, the senator seemed hellbent on self-destruction. He'd have to find a way to keep him in line. Keep them from both going down.

And Ed had no intention of going down. Not now. Not when he'd just discovered this new side of himself.

He'd used shorted electrical wiring to disguise the arsons. He was good, but there were only so many of these incidents he could explain away in such a short period of time.

He was damned lucky they'd gotten away with what they had.

The senator was losing it. Sooner or later, he was going to really fuck it up and Ed wouldn't be able to help him. He just had to make sure the senator didn't bring him down with him.

Maybe the guy wasn't crazy. Could be drugs. Wouldn't be the first time someone in a position like that was an addict.

But it didn't matter. What mattered was that Ed was going to find a way to come out of this ahead.

14

Casper fire fighter Brendan Mercer couldn't ignore the feeling deep in the pit of his stomach. There was something *wrong* with the prostitute fires. They were too similar to be accidents. And they were being wrapped up too quickly and cleanly. They just didn't sit right with him.

And the last two, they were too professional, too clinical. Either the guy had suddenly figured out a better way to burn the scene, or they had had help from someone who knew what they were doing. As much as he did not want to think about those implications, he couldn't ignore them.

He needed to talk to the chief.

Just before his shift ended, he knocked on the chief's door.

"Brendan, come on in," Ed said, waving him in.

"I'm sorry to bother you, sir."

"Nonsense. What can I do for you?"

"These fires lately, with the uh, prostitutes, I think we're missing something. Something important."

Brendan saw something dark flash across his chief's face before he quickly got it under control.

"What do you mean?" his boss asked.

Brendan ran a hand through his hair. "It's like a serial killer or something. And we're just writing them off as random accidents."

"It bothers you?" the chief asked.

"It does. I wanted to get your take on it."

"Sure, I'm swamped here right now, but I'll stop by your place on the way home. We can talk then."

"Thank you, sir."

The chief walked him to the door, put a hand on his shoulder. "Don't worry. We'll figure it out."

ED CURSED under his breath as Brendan left his office. One more damn problem he had to deal with.

After work, he drove straight to Brendan's house. It could turn out to be nothing, but he'd mentally prepared himself on the way over to do whatever needed to be done.

He noted with pleasure that Brendan appeared to have had at least one drink already when he opened the front door, slightly unsteady on his feet. Could make things easier if worse came to worse.

"Chief," Brendan said. "Drink?" he asked, pouring himself another glass of Scotch from the open bottle on the counter.

Ed shook his head. "I'm good, thank you. Now tell me what's on your mind."

Brendan took a deep drink. Shook his head. "I don't want to believe it, but I think one of us set those fires."

"Why?"

"The last couple are too damned good. Too clean. An average person wouldn't know how to do that."

"You have any proof of this?"

Brendan slowly shook his head.

Ed studied the other man. The way Brendan was looking at him. Like he *knew*. "It's not what you think," he said.

"Then what is it? Because what I'm seeing here, it doesn't add up, Chief."

Brendan was too smart for his own good. Ed sighed. And it would be the end of him.

"Tell me I'm wrong." Brendan was practically *begging* him to deny it.

Damnit, he didn't *want* to do it. Brendan was part of his family, a brother in every way except blood. But it was a sacrifice that needed to be made. He'd stage it just right, a slow burning backdraft to limit the damage.

Brendan was still looking at him. "Come here," Ed motioned him forward. "I'll explain everything."

"You were right," Ed whispered. He felt no remorse as he snapped the other man's neck. It wasn't his fault the younger man was so damned trusting. He had seen it in the younger man's eyes, how much he wanted to believe the evidence was wrong. It was touching how much faith Brendan'd had in him.

He drug the body to the bottom of the stairs and stepped back, eying the scene. Yes, he could work with this.

FIREFIGHTER THOMAS McGAVIN listened in disbelief as their chief finished the briefing informing them the following Monday that one of their own was dead.

And not just one of their own. Brendan. One that Thomas had considered a friend. A good friend.

Dead in a fire. At his home.

He turned his attention back to the chief. "All indications are it was an accidental death. He had a high blood alcohol content and appears to have fallen down the stairs. There was an unattended pot on the stove that eventually caught fire."

He tuned out the rest of the words, then went through the day on auto pilot.

Late that night, he lay in bed unable to sleep. A week ago, he would have accepted Brendan's death as an accident, no questions asked.

But four nights ago, he and Brendan had gone out for a drink. His friend had been troubled. It had taken a couple drinks before he'd opened up. He closed his eyes, remembering the conversation.

"Something's not right with those fires with the dead prostitutes. I have this feeling that the chief knows more than he's letting on."

"That's a pretty serious accusation."

Brendan ran a hand down his face. "I know. It's probably nothing. I'll talk to him, figure out what's going on."

And now Brendan was dead.

Was it just a coincidence or something much more sinister?

He rolled over, knowing sleep would not come.

THOMAS WENT to work early the next morning. After saying hello to the few people in the building, he grabbed a cup of coffee and made his way down the hall. He paused in front of the chief's office. No one was around. He slowly opened the door.

He didn't think about what he was doing, just crossed the room to the chief's desk.

Not sure what he was looking for, he carefully but quickly looked through the paperwork on top of the desk, then one by one went through the drawers.

In the middle drawer, he saw a charred business card in a plastic bag. He glanced at the hall, found it still empty, then looked back at the card. *Senator Westmoreland.*

What the hell?

He quickly put the card back and exited the office.

He went outside and pulled out his cell phone. *No.* Then they would have his name and number. He needed to make an anonymous call. But how? It wasn't like there was a damned phone booth down the street.

There was an unused office next to the chief's. He quickly headed inside, shut the door, and picked up the phone.

"Casper police department," a gruff voice answered.

"I want to report a possible crime. I think our fire chief is conspiring with Senator Westmoreland. I think they might have something to do with the prostitute fires."

"Your, name, sir?"

Thomas hung up.

FIFTEEN MINUTES LATER, Police Chief Delaney pulled the burner phone out of his desk, hit the one speed-dial number he'd programmed into it.

"You better have a damned good reason for calling me," the senator said when he answered.

"Look, I've been nothing but loyal to you. So drop the fucking attitude. I wouldn't have called if I didn't have a damned good reason."

"What is it?"

"There's a firefighter asking questions about you and the fire chief."

"Give me the name," the senator said.

"I don't have a name, but he called from a phone inside the fire house."

The senator hung up, then immediately dialed the phone again.

"You've got a hell of a mess to clean up," he said when Ed answered the phone.

15

It didn't take Ed long to figure out who'd made the call to the police. Thomas McGavin had been Brendan's best friend. And he'd been acting off for the last few days. Now Ed just needed an opportunity to eliminate this new threat.

He'd thought about another fire. But that would be too suspicious. No. There had to be another way.

Thomas lived several miles out of town on an isolated road. Ed smiled as he pictured the steep hill leading up Thomas's road. Lucky for him, Ed's dad had been a mechanic and he had many fond memories of working with his dad on numerous makes and models of cars as he grew up. He'd learned a lot from his old man.

And he planned on putting that knowledge to good use now.

He called his wife and told her he'd be pulling an overnight shift. She was used to it and asked no questions. Hell, he was sure she was perfectly happy to park her ass on the couch and watch reality TV without him.

At two in the morning, he parked a quarter mile from Thomas's place. He quickly but silently made his way towards the house on foot. There was no garage, just a one-story cabin. There were no lights on, no visible movement inside the cabin or out.

Damn, this was going to be too easy, Ed thought as he made his way through the trees towards Thomas's white Ford F250 parked in the driveway.

Fifteen minutes later, he was back in his own car and headed back to the station.

He was at his desk when the call came in later that morning. *Bad car accident. Possible fatality. Vehicle on fire.* He fought down a smile, forced a serious expression on his face as he ran out of his office.

"Two dead firefighters in a week?" Hoyt asked Sanderson that morning as they gathered in Sanderson's office. "What the hell is going on?"

Sanderson shrugged as he shuffled papers around on his desk. "Might be a coincidence. This one was a car crash."

"The guy's brakes failed," Hoyt said, head cocked to the side.

"It happens." Sanderson paused. "Look, I'm not saying it isn't suspicious. But we won't know if the car was tampered with for at least a day. We may never know. The car and body were both burned to a crisp."

"Exactly my point," Hoyt said.

Sanderson didn't say a word, just sighed, clearly frustrated.

"Let's all just relax," Ang said. "What can we do, right now?"

"We need to talk to the fire chief," Hoyt said.

"Have at it," Sanderson said, looking up from his desk.

Hoyt turned to Ang. "Let's go."

"So, what exactly are we going to do at the fire station?" Ang asked as Hoyt drove across town.

"Talk to the chief. Then ask the guys about the prostitute fires, the recent deaths of two of their own. See if anyone has anything interesting to say."

"Okay," Ang said as Hoyt parked the car.

The chief ushered them into his office. The guy looked exhausted, with red-rimmed eyes.

"Sorry, please have a seat," he said after a minute. "It's been a hell of a few days."

They sat. "I know it's a bad time," Hoyt said. "We just need to know if there's a reason beyond coincidence linking the deaths of two of your men."

The chief shook his head. "I wish I had an easy answer for you. But as devastating as it has been for our firehouse, it's just a series of unfortunate events."

Hoyt stood, knowing he'd get nothing else out of the chief. "We'll spend a little while talking to your men, then we'll be on our way."

Ed stood as well. "Thank you for coming. I wish I could be more help to you."

He muttered a curse as he watched the two agents walk down the hall. He knew they wouldn't get anything from his men, but he didn't like their presence in his firehouse.

HOYT AND ANG kept it informal, talking to the group as a whole, not pulling them in individually for interviews. Hoyt gave a brief overview and asked if anyone had anything they thought could help to talk to them. Then he and Ang set up on opposite sides of the station, letting people come to them.

Hoyt felt the strange unfamiliar stirrings of jealousy seeing a young fireman hitting shamelessly on Ang. What the hell? She was his partner. Nothing more. At least that's what he kept telling himself.

And yet, as he shot a withering glare at the guy, he took a great deal of satisfaction as the guy backed away.

Ang raised an eyebrow and he shrugged.

Was it possible for a man like John Hoyt to be jealous? She shot him another curious glance, but Hoyt was already walking out the door. Damn. She couldn't get a handle on that man.

She followed him to the car. "Did you get anything good?" she asked, after she'd buckled in.

Hoyt shrugged. "Some speculation. Nothing concrete."

He turned his attention to the road.

Hoyt was angry at himself. He knew he was being an ass, ignoring Ang. He was acting like a damned high school jock when the rival team leered at his head cheerleader. Ang wasn't his. Not by a long shot. She was his partner, yes, and they were sleeping together, but he had no claim to her beyond that. He told himself being protective came with the territory. Of course he would look after her best interests. That was part of the job.

And he was a goddamned liar.

He wanted her and didn't want anyone else to have her.

This was going to be a problem. And he had no idea what to do about it.

WARD WAS in Sanderson's office when they got back to the RA. Hoyt thought he looked tired. But running back and forth between Casper and Cheyenne dealing with two very complicated cases couldn't be easy.

"Anything good?" Sanderson asked.

Hoyt shrugged and Ang remained silent.

Ward looked between the two of them. "Okay, then. A dead end. On a different note, I have to fly back to Denver tonight. Some damned meeting I can't get out of. I should be able to come back out in a day or two."

"I'll take you," Hoyt said.

Ward nodded and started gathering his things.

"How's it going in Cheyenne?" Hoyt asked as they got into the car.

"Not well," Ward said, looking straight ahead, his tone of voice and dark scowl clearly conveying that he didn't want to talk about it.

Hoyt shut up and started the car.

He could feel his boss looking at him as they neared the airport. "What?" he asked.

"I know I don't need to remind you what an amazing woman Ang is. And I know it's not easy for you, but if you want her be more than your partner, you need to get your head out of your ass."

Hoyt laughed. He couldn't help it. "Tell me something I don't know," he said.

Ward relaxed back into his seat. "You'll figure it out."

Hoyt sure as fuck hoped so, because he had a feeling he'd be miserable without her.

THE NEXT MORNING, Hoyt was surprised to find Ang at their normal breakfast table. He grabbed a cup of coffee, filled his plate, and joined her. Before he could come up with anything to say, she smiled.

"I was an ass. Again," he said.

She nodded. "You were."

He wanted to explain it to her. "This case, it's getting to me. And I'm struggling with being a partner and -"

She cut him off. "I get it. I'm struggling too. We just have to struggle together. It'll make things easier."

Hoyt let out a breath, wondering yet again, what he'd done to deserve this amazing woman being in his life. "You're right."

"I know." She smiled again.

After they'd finished eating, Hoyt focused his thoughts on work. "Brendan, the firefighter that died in the home fire, his funeral is today. I was thinking we should go, see what we can see."

"Won't hurt," she said.

ANG SAT NEXT to Hoyt in a pew at the back of the small Catholic church where Brendan Mercer was being laid to rest. Despite the somber occasion, she hadn't been able to ignore how good John Hoyt looked in a suit. Dressed or undressed, the man had an effect on her that she couldn't seem to control.

She forced herself to pay attention. Not to what the priest was saying, but to the other people gathered there. She didn't see anything or anyone out of place.

She and Hoyt both watched intently as the fire chief moved to the front of the church to speak.

Hoyt narrowed his eyes. The words the chief spoke were appropriate, but something was off about this guy. It was in his eyes as he looked up at the crowd as he gave the eulogy. There was a spark of pride there. No sorrow.

As soon as the funeral was over, Hoyt had his cell phone out. "The fire chief, Edmund Newkirk. I want everything you can find on him," he said to Ward.

Ang shot him a curious look but didn't say anything until they were in the car. "What's going on?" she asked.

Hoyt shook his head. "I can't explain it, but I think Newkirk is our guy. The key to solving this."

She knew Hoyt's reputation, trusted his instincts. They knew the fire chief had to be involved somehow. But this sudden sense of urgency from Hoyt seemed to come out of left field. He must have seen something that she'd missed.

"Okay," she said.

He raised an eyebrow. "Just like that?"

She shrugged. "You're my partner. I trust you. I know your reputation. If you say there's something there, there's something there."

He held her eyes for a long minute. "Thank you," he said softly.

She smiled. "You're welcome. Just don't make me regret it."

Her faith in him was humbling.

He shouldn't be surprised. She'd been nothing but a loyal partner from the start of the case. But they *were* sleeping together. And sex tended to complicate things.

He shook his head. *He* needed to stop complicating things with this line of thinking. "Okay. Let's go back to the hotel, regroup, and see where this leads."

"Sounds good," Ang said, leaning her head back.

"A fire chief and a United States Senator? What an odd combination," Hoyt said a few miles later. "Add in a corrupt police chief and it's a hell of a mess."

"Crazy attracts crazy?" Ang asked.

"Something like that," Hoyt said.

16

Two more days passed with very little progress in their case. Hoyt was frustrated. Not just with the case, but with his feelings for Ang. This was new territory for him. And he knew he was probably fucking it up. Again.

They'd come back to her hotel room after dinner. He watched her across the room as she worked on her laptop.

He was painfully aware of her presence, her soft feminine scent. Who the fuck knew the scent of lavender could turn him on so much? This was why he couldn't work like this; he couldn't afford to worry about someone. It interfered with the job. He tried to explain it to her, knew he was failing miserably.

She raised her gaze to meet his. "What is it?" she asked, getting up and standing next to him. "What's wrong?"

He tucked a strand of hair behind her ear, the tender gesture out of character for him. "I have a feeling this case is going to get more dangerous before it's over. And I worry. For your safety."

"I don't need you to worry about me. I know my job, I'm good at it, and I can handle myself."

"I know that, dammit."

She stepped closer. "So, what's the problem?"

His chest constricted painfully as he stared at her and he struggled to breathe. He needed to get away from her before it killed him. "I've got to go. I'll see you in the morning."

"Dammit, Hoyt. What is wrong with you?"

"How the hell am I supposed to get any work done if I want to screw your brains out every time I see you?"

"Screw my brains out? God, you are *so* romantic."

He couldn't look her in the eye, it hurt too damned much. "I won't apologize for who I am. I'm not good with relationships, that's why I try to avoid them." He paused. "The truth is, I can't seem to get a handle on what I'm feeling for you. So if I seem crude, I don't mean to be." He forced himself to look her in the eye now. She'd earned his trust, his respect. His love. *Holy fuck. He was falling in love with her.* He opened his mouth but no words came out.

Ang was touched; it was probably as close to an apology as she would get from a man like him. "I know that must have been hard for you to say."

"You have no idea." He gave her a half-smile.

"We're consenting adults. Why is this so difficult for you?" she asked.

"What do you want me to say? You want to hear about how my dad was an alcoholic? How my mom let him beat her up every night? How as soon as I was strong enough, I beat the shit out of him and ran away? That I joined the Navy as soon as I was old enough, where I did things you don't even want to know about. I'm comfortable with violence, it's all I know." He paused with his eyes flashing. "Or maybe you want to know that in all my life, I've never wanted anything as much as I want you, and it scares the hell out of me."

He was breathing hard, his chest heaving up and down. He never opened up like this. Never. What in the hell was wrong with him?

It took a lot to shock Ang, but she was shocked now and all she could do was stand and stare at him. Her lower lip started to tremble. No declarations of love had ever affected her as much as his words. She hadn't acknowledged how deep her own feelings for him ran until that very moment. It startled her. And brought tears to her eyes.

Hoyt couldn't stand the intense emotions he saw on her face and started to back away.

"Hoyt."

He stopped.

"Don't you think I'm scared too?" Her voice was barely a whisper. "But, I'm willing to take the risk and see where this leads. We'll just take it slowly."

He turned around and stepped closer until they were almost touching. "Are you sure about this?"

"No, but I'm willing to try."

"Well, hell, let's give it a try." His shoulders relaxed and his lips curved into a smile as he bent down to kiss her.

THE CHANGE between them after they cleared the air was amazing to Ang. Things between them seemed easier. Progress on the case was still slow, but she was enjoying the long nights in the hotel room with him going over their notes, planning their next step, then making love. It was going way beyond casual sex. But they didn't talk about the future. She supposed neither of them were ready to think about what would happen after the case ended.

She hated that Hoyt's childhood had been so tragic. Hers had been the opposite. Yes, she came from a family of tough law enforcement officers and her parent's hadn't been together in a long time, but it was a big, loving family. And she ached for the part of Hoyt that had missed out on that.

She sighed and leaned back against the couch, tucking her feet under her, focusing back on the case. "I feel like we're taking one step forward and two back. Again."

"Yeah." Hoyt rubbed his forehead. "It's late. Let's call it for tonight."

Ang closed her eyes. Then opened them quickly when she felt Hoyt reaching for her foot and pulling it towards him.

"What are you doing?" she asked.

"Just relax," he said as he started rubbing the arch of her foot.

She closed her eyes again and tried not to moan as he continued massaging her foot. Who knew the badass former Navy SEAL could give a foot rub?

After he finished her other foot, she felt boneless and totally relaxed. "That was amazing. Thank you."

He smiled. "My pleasure."

"Let me return the favor."

His grin turned wicked.

"With a back rub," she said, swatting his knee. "Sit down in front of me."

He complied and she started massaging the tight muscles in his shoulders. Soon, she felt him relax. She marveled at how things had changed with him. How . . . domestic it felt.

She ran her hands down to his chest. "Now about that other favor," she whispered in his ear.

He quickly pulled her down on the floor with him.

BEING with Ang was too easy. They were so in tune with each other. They followed each other's leads perfectly.

It was amazing to Hoyt how well they worked together. They certainly had different ways of working a case, but their ideas meshed perfectly, their styles complimenting each other. Their nonverbal communication was as good as he'd had with anyone in the SEALs. But despite making a damned good team, Hoyt still worried about Ang. His head knew she was a strong, smart, capable federal agent. His heart saw her as a beautiful, tiny, woman he cared a great deal about.

In his heart, he knew he loved her. There was no denying it.

Yeah, Lash had called it, he was pretty much fucked. And he had no idea what to do about it.

He didn't know how to have a relationship with a woman. It was completely foreign to him.

It was so much easier to work with men. No emotional bullshit.

No walking on eggshells. And yet, there was no question in his mind that Ang was a damned good agent.

He was just too emotionally attached to her. But it wasn't like he could stop now and take it back. That train had left the station long ago. Maybe not from the first moment he'd met her, but at least from the car ride to Casper. She'd gotten to him, gotten deep inside. And he didn't know if he could let her go.

He didn't want to.

But they were in the middle of a case. What would happen when they were at home? He'd never lived with a woman. These past few weeks with Ang had been the closest he'd ever come. Was what they had sustainable long term?

He knew they'd have a lot to figure out once this case was over. And that didn't look like it would be anytime soon. They'd just have to focus on the present and see what happened after that.

17

A ng refused to think about what would happen after the case was over. It was too easy to just enjoy living in the moment. Despite moving forward with their relationship, she and Hoyt had never really talked about the future. And how could they until they'd solved the case?

The holidays were coming up soon. Would they spend them together? Would the case even be over by then? Too many questions and no answers.

She knew it was possible for agents to successfully have a relationship together and be successful at their jobs. But wasn't it too soon to think about that with Hoyt? She'd only known him for a few weeks. And she didn't exactly have the best track record when it came to relationships. And she was pretty damned sure Hoyt didn't either.

And yet, she couldn't ignore the way she felt with him. He awakened parts of her she'd never acknowledged. He made her think about white picket fences and two point two kids.

She shook her head. Wondered if she was going insane. Just because they had spectacular sex and were damned good partners didn't mean it should be anything other than that. She needed to be realistic. So they should just enjoy it as long as it lasted. No need to complicate things.

ON THE AGENDA the next afternoon was another conference call in Sanderson's office. As soon as they walked in, Sanderson hit the button on the speaker phone.

"Any new leads?" Ward asked.

"Not much," Hoyt answered, unable to keep he frustration out of his voice. "We've gone through property records, and the fire chief owns a small cabin north of town in addition to his house in Casper. And there's been talk of an old clothing factory on the edge of town being used to store drugs, but we've been unable to confirm anything."

"Sanderson's people searched the factory two weeks ago and found nothing," Ang added.

"Search it again," Ward said. "Drive by the cabin first, then hit the factory. I'm at the airport now. I'll be there by the time you're done."

"Yes, sir," Hoyt answered and ended the call.

Ang looked at the clock. It was four-fifteen.

Hoyt shrugged. "No time like the present."

"Okay, then," Ang said. "Let's do it."

"Have fun. I'll pick our boss up," Sanderson said.

FORTY MINUTES LATER, Ang looked out the window as they slowly drove by the fire chief's run-down looking cabin outside of town. It definitely didn't look like much.

Hoyt slowed down and spent a long time looking at the property.

"What?" Ang asked.

"Isolated. Only one way in. Good place to hide out," he said.

Ang shrugged. "Doesn't look like anyone's been there for a while."

"Yeah," Hoyt said, heading back to the main road and then towards the factory. But he didn't sound convinced.

· · ·

"THERE'S NOTHING HERE," Ang said with a sigh. They'd just spent two hours searching the abandoned factory on the edge of town with nothing to show for it. Unless you counted ancient sewing machines, moldy fabric, and empty storage rooms.

Hoyt ran a hand down his face. "I know." The back of his neck felt itchy. They were missing something.

He paused, listening. All he could hear was the sound of their breathing, but still, there was *something*. Something that was very wrong. His instincts were on full alert now.

He smelled it an instant before she did. Smoke.

Their eyes met in alarm.

"We've got to get out of here. Now." He grabbed her hand as the ceiling groaned and creaked above them. He estimated the distance to the front door at three hundred feet. *Fuck.* They weren't going to make it.

But there was no other way out of the old building. "Run," he said, urging her forward, pushing her in front of him.

Ang ran, ignoring the acrid smell of smoke. She couldn't see the fire yet, but she could hear and feel the subtle signs of its presence around them.

She heard an explosion overhead, then Hoyt pushed her to the floor, throwing his body down on top of her. She hit the floor hard, knocking the breath out of her lungs. There was a rush of heat and pain as the roof started caving in around them.

Her eyes were burning and she struggled to take a breath. "Hoyt." His weight was crushing her but he didn't move. "John." There was no response. *Jesus, don't let him be dead.* She struggled to roll his body off her.

He was unconscious, but alive, his chest moving slowly up and down. There was a deep gash on the back of his head and blood was soaking through his shirt on the left side.

"John! Wake up!" She coughed and flinched as another beam from the ceiling crashed down next to them. Sweat stung her eyes. She grabbed him under the arms and started pulling him towards the entrance.

The effort strained her already burning lungs, but step by agonizing step, she made her way through the flames and smoke, ignoring the pain as she felt the hair on her arms start to singe. But she was not leaving without Hoyt.

She burst through the door into the fresh air and dropped to the ground, coughing, gasping for breath. Hoyt groaned beside her and she felt relief surge through her as his eyes opened and focused on her.

She pulled her gun, looked around and saw no one, nothing out of place. She turned back towards Hoyt.

"The car . . . have to get there . . . building . . . going to go," he managed between coughs.

"Jesus." She struggled to her feet, pulling him up with her and together they limped towards the car.

She helped him into the passenger seat, then jumped in and gunned the engine.

They had just pulled out onto the main road when the explosion rocked the countryside behind them.

"How you doing?" she asked. Her eyes flicked away from the road. Hoyt was slumped in the passenger seat, eyes closed, holding his side.

"I've been better." He opened his eyes, and seeing her look of concern added, "But I've been worse."

Her eyes darted to the rearview mirror. She could see flashing lights in the distance, but no one appeared to be following them. She turned onto the next side road and pulled over, then took off her jacket and pushed it against Hoyt's side, then turned on the interior light. He was quiet, too quiet.

"I don't like this head wound and you've lost a lot of blood," she said.

"I'll be okay."

"Stop playing the goddamned hero." She grabbed her phone, pulled up a map. "We're only twenty minutes away from the hospital." She scrolled through her contacts. "I'll have Ward meet us there." She put the car in gear and stepped hard on the gas as she waited for Ward to pick up.

The fact that Hoyt didn't argue about going to the hospital drove home how serious his condition was. She pushed down harder on the gas pedal.

"Calhoun." Her boss's voice echoed through her phone.

"It's Agent Nobles. There was a fire at the factory we were checking out north of town. Hoyt's hurt. We're headed to the hospital."

"On my way," Ward said.

By the time she pulled to a stop in front of the hospital's emergency entrance fifteen minutes later, Ang was scared. Hoyt was unresponsive and extremely pale, and there was blood all over the car. She opened the door and screamed at the green-clad figures rushing towards them, "We need a doctor, now!"

She flashed her badge, then stood back as they got Hoyt out of the car and onto a stretcher. He was quickly whisked out of her view.

She followed the doctors into the hospital where they tried to persuade her to see a nurse. "We need to get a look at your arms," one of them said as she pushed her way past them.

The burns were starting to throb and she felt dizzy and weak. The adrenaline rush was dying out, leaving pain and fear for Hoyt. "All right," she finally agreed, following the nurse. "All right. But I want to know the instant they're done looking at him."

WARD STUCK his head inside the curtain of the exam room just as the nurse was finishing bandaging her arms.

"You must have broken a few speed limits," Ang muttered.

"Glad you still have your sense of humor," he said with a raised brow.

She tried to smile, shrugged a shoulder.

Ward nodded in understanding. "I saw the doctor. Hoyt's going to be fine. He lost quite a bit of blood and has a mild concussion, but he's okay."

Relief flooded through her. She felt the sting of tears and had to take a deep steadying breath, pressing her fingers against her eyes. "I was worried. He didn't look so good when we got here." She paused, voice shaking. "He was trying to protect me."

The nurse finished and Ward led her to the waiting room. "Are you ready to talk about it?"

She nodded.

Ward got out his notepad and they moved towards a quiet corner of the room.

She walked her boss through every step of their day's events. "I don't understand. Everything was uneventful until the fire. No one followed us there."

Ward sighed. "Their could have been an incendiary device set before you got there. There could have been a motion sensor or video camera that picked up your arrival."

"Was there any sign of that?"

"The building's a total loss. Any evidence that was there is long gone. There's nothing left," he said, rubbing a hand across his forehead.

She nodded. "Damn. We just can't catch a break."

"We're going to get him," Ward assured her.

She nodded, unable to trust her voice.

"We will," Ward said, squeezing her shoulder as he left the room.

BY THE TIME they let her in to see Hoyt, he was sitting up in the bed. His head was shaved and bandaged. His shirt was off, another larger bandage on his side.

"You're hurt," was the first thing he said as she entered the room.

She looked down at her bandaged arms and shrugged. "Just minor burns. You're looking better."

His face grew serious. "You saved my life, you know."

She shook her head. "You were the one who pushed me out of the way."

"But you got me out of there."

She forced a smile. "I guess we're even then."

He gave her a half-smile, half-grunt. He was still marveling at how someone her size had managed to carry his dead weight the distance she had.

She sat down on the edge of the bed, put a hand on his leg. "Ward wants you to take it easy for a while."

"Like hell. I'm ready to go now."

"No, you're not. You lost a hell of a lot of blood, all over the car I might add. You need to get some rest. I'll see you tomorrow morning."

She gave him a quick kiss on the lips, then turned around before she let the tears fall.

In the hall, she leaned back against the wall, fighting exhaustion. She felt weak and shaky with relief. She'd been so worried about him. But he was fine. And of course he wouldn't take any time off. Damned stubborn man.

Hoyt watched her walk out the door of his hospital room. Today had been too goddamned close. He was used to dealing with danger, but the thought of anything happening to Ang was not acceptable to him. He needed to bring this case to an end. And he needed to do it yesterday.

As much as he wanted to get the hell out of there and back to work now, his exhausted and battered body wouldn't let him. He knew all too well how far he could push himself and knew there was nothing he could do until he rested. He'd fall flat on his face if he tried to leave now.

But in the morning, he was getting the fuck out of the damned hospital and stopping these sons of bitches. Even if it killed him.

ED LOOKED DOWN at his vibrating phone, cursed silently, then answered.

"They're still alive."

There was no way Ed could mistake the anger in the senator's words. But he wasn't going to apologize. He'd done nothing wrong. The fire he'd staged at the factory had been perfect. No one should have been able to make it out alive. The damned FBI Agents seemed to have nine lives. "I'll fix it."

"Damn right, you will. They're getting too close. We need them gone. Now. They can't keep sniffing around."

"What do you want me to do?"

"Take them out, like I told you."

Like it was that easy to kill two FBI agents. "You can't be serious. We need to wait a while."

"Do you want to spend the rest of your life in prison? Because I sure as hell don't intend to," Westmoreland said. "Make it happen."

Ed cursed at the silent phone. He could make it happen all right. He just hated that he was the one that always seemed to be putting his ass on the line.

He needed a drink. Needed to think.

"Everything okay?" his wife asked from the living room doorway as he grabbed his coat and headed for the front door.

"Yeah, I'm just going out for a bit."

A worried look briefly crossed her face before she forced a smile. "Okay, I'll have dinner ready when you get back."

"Sounds good." He gave her a quick kiss on the cheek and was out the door.

Fifteen minutes later, he was sitting in the dark of his favorite bar, a glass of bourbon in front of him.

His back was up against the wall. Murdering fucking FBI agents? That was never part of his agreement with the senator. He drained his glass, signaled the waitress for another.

He took a drink, welcomed the subtle burn. Fuck Westmoreland. This shit had to stop. Right now. He'd head to his cabin and clear out the evidence from the fires he'd set.

Could evil corrupt? Could it have rubbed off on him from Senator Westmoreland? Or did one wrong deed pave the way to greater ones? He took another drink. The answers really didn't matter. What mattered was that he liked who he was becoming. Liked his new power. And he'd do anything to keep it. That was the bottom line.

But then what? He didn't have enough money saved to disappear. Didn't have evidence to take to the cops. He ran through the limited options in his head. But he was so much stronger now and capable of so much more than he'd ever realized before he'd started this journey.

He'd have to kill Westmoreland. There was no other option. No other way out of this damned mess.

He laughed. Just a few short months ago the thought of killing a United States Senator would have seemed absurd. Now, it was the most logical thought he'd had in a long time.

He finished his drink, then went home and ate the meatloaf and mashed potatoes his wife had made.

18

Ang didn't like the look in Hoyt's eyes the next morning when she walked into his hospital room. With the newly-shaved head and dangerous look in his eyes, he looked downright scary. She had a quick glimpse of what he must have been like when he was in the SEALs.

He was already out of bed and dressed at 8 am, arms crossed, waiting for her. He didn't look weak anymore. His face was set and determined. "I want this over," he said, as he glared over at her. "Let's go."

"Good morning to you, too," she mumbled.

A nurse arrived, pushing a wheelchair through the door.

"Fuck that," Hoyt said.

"It's hospital rules," the nurse said.

Hoyt just glared at her and walked out of the room.

"Sorry," Ang said as she hurried past the nurse and into the hall.

"Would you slow down?" she called after Hoyt.

He stopped, his entire body tense. He took a deep breath as she caught up to him. "I need to get the hell out of here." He ran a shaky hand down his stubble covered face.

"Okay." She nodded and led the way outside and to their car.

Thankfully, Ward had arranged to have it cleaned the night before, so there was no trace left of Hoyt's blood inside.

She shivered, not sure if it was because of the chill in the air or thinking about Hoyt's blood all over the car. She turned up the heater.

"How are you feeling?" she asked as she pulled out of the parking lot.

"I'm fine," he said, staring out the passenger window.

He didn't say another word on the drive back to the hotel.

"Do you want to meet with Ward?" she asked as they walked into the hotel lobby.

"Later. I've got some things I need to do. I'll catch up with you guys later."

They got into the elevator and rode up to their rooms in silence. He barely looked at her as she got off the elevator on her floor.

Ang let herself into her room and sighed. *What the hell?* It felt like he was shutting her out. And it fucking hurt.

Maybe he was just in pain and needed to be by himself for a while. She wished she believed that, but she knew better. She'd never figure him out.

But damned if she didn't want to try.

Hoyt let his door slam shut behind him. *Damn, I fucking hate hospitals.* He knew he'd been cold to Ang. But dammit, he couldn't let her get hurt. No fucking way was he going to let that happen. The day before had shown just how desperate these guys were. They wouldn't think twice about killing either of them. And he was not going to risk Ang's life.

He couldn't. She meant too much.

As much as it hurt, he had to put aside his feelings for her, and he knew he was acting like a caveman, but there it was. He shouldn't have let himself get that close to her. It had been a mistake, but he didn't have it left in him to regret it. Not one single moment of his

time with her. It had all been more than he'd deserved. Now he had
to get them both out of this alive.

The painkillers were wearing off and his head was throbbing. He
downed a handful of ibuprofen and fired up his computer. If he had
to shut her out to keep her safe, so be it.

THE MORE ANG thought about Hoyt's behavior, the more pissed off
she got. No matter what their personal feelings were, they were partners. They needed to work together to solve this case. And despite
what Hoyt might think, he couldn't do it all on his own. Especially
injured.

Why did he have to be so goddamned stubborn? Why did she
have to care so much?

She grabbed her keycard and headed to his room.

He was not going to shut her out. Not when he needed her the
most.

HOYT HEARD the knock on his door, looked out the peephole at Ang
and sighed. He did not want to deal with this right now. He didn't
have the strength to keep her at arms length. Not now.

Ang pounded on the door again. "Hoyt, I know you're in there.
Open the damned door or I'll let myself in."

He opened the door and stepped out of the way. She looked like a
tiny tornado.

Her eyes flashed with anger he knew he deserved. "You do not get
to treat me like that." She pointed a finger at his chest. "I'm your *partner*. And your lover. You may think you're protecting me by shutting
me out, but it doesn't work that way. And oh, by the way, you're the one
that ended up hurt and in the hospital." She stopped, breathing hard.

Hoyt closed his eyes. She was right. He knew she was right. And
damned if her calling him on his bullshit didn't turn him on. He
opened his eyes, searching for how to explain his feelings to her.

"Well, I see that got through to you," she said sarcastically. She turned to go.

Hoyt grabbed her arm before she got to the door, spinning her back around to face him. His eyes searched hers. Then his mouth was crushing hers. And despite everything said and unsaid, Ang couldn't stop her body from responding to his.

She got lost in the physical sensations as he roughly stripped off both of their clothes and shoved her down onto the bed. She couldn't control her response to this man, no matter how pissed off she was at him. It wasn't until her hand ran along the bandage on his side that she pulled back. "Your stitches," she said.

"Are fine," he growled.

Then he was inside her and all she could think about was how damned good it felt.

WARD HIT his alarm clock and sighed. It was amazing how fast six a.m. came. Five minutes later, room service knocked on his door. With his entire morning packed full of conference calls, he wouldn't be leaving his room anytime soon.

He left the food on the table and carried a cup of coffee to the bathroom, hoping a shower would wake him up. He turned the temperature to hot and drank some of his coffee while the bathroom filled with steam.

He knew he could have stayed in Denver or sent someone else to Casper. But he still liked getting out in the field. And as good as he believed Hoyt and Ang to be, this case was a damned tricky one. And he wanted to help them solve it.

But first, he'd have to handle the calls and trying to run the Denver Field Office from a hotel room.

Promptly at eight, Ang knocked on his door.

He opened it and let her in. "Where's Hoyt?" Both agents were supposed to be on the first call with him.

Ang gave an annoyed shrug. "He wanted to meet with Sanderson first thing."

Ward could see that Ang wasn't happy about Hoyt's decision. "Look, Hoyt has his own way of doing things. I know it's frustrating. But I see how good you are for each other. Just be patient and give him some space when he needs it."

She gave him a skeptical look, but kept her mouth shut.

He poured her a cup of coffee. "Now, let's update the crew back home."

She took the coffee and nodded. "Sounds good."

SANDERSON WATCHED Hoyt pace back and forth across the small conference room. He could almost see the waves of anger radiating off the man.

Finally, Hoyt turned and leveled his gaze on him. "We've got to find a way to fucking end this. *Now.*"

"We're doing everything we can. You know that."

Hoyt turned and started pacing again, running a hand over his newly shaved head, stopping at the nasty looking scab on the back of his scalp.

Sanderson had a good idea what was going on in the other agent's head. "Look, I get that you're worried about her, but you have to let shit that go. We all have to do our job."

Hoyt whirled around. "You don't know what the hell you're talking about."

"So this has nothing to do with Agent Nobles?" Sanderson asked calmly.

Hoyt sighed.

"Look, I'm tired of this shit, too. It's happening in my own fucking backyard and I haven't been able to stop it."

"I know," Hoyt said. "But you and I, we've been there, done that, got the damned war medals to prove it. But *she* hasn't. I need to make sure she's safe."

"And I know I'm stating the obvious here, but she knew the dangers of the job when she signed up."

Hoyt shook his head. "You got a woman?"

Sanderson shook his head.

"I don't even know how the fuck it happened, but she *got* to me."

"Then don't screw it up. Let her in. Let her do her job."

Hoyt put his hands on his hips. "I don't know if I can."

"Then let's figure out how to end this."

"What else can we do?"

Sanderson cocked his head. "How do you feel about doing some UC work?"

"Undercover as what?"

"Not sure yet. Let's brainstorm with Ward."

Hoyt shrugged. "Worth a shot. Let's do it."

An hour later, they had a plan.

Five hours later, Ang stood in Sanderson's office, hands on her hips, waiting for Hoyt to come out of the bathroom.

Her mouth fell open when he came back into the room. She quickly closed it. "Jesus, you stink," she said.

"Where *did* you get these clothes?" Hoyt asked Sanderson.

The other agent shrugged. "Thrift store. Then I left them in the dumpster for a while, spilled some vodka on them."

Hoyt looked down at his ensemble. "I really don't want to know what those stains are."

Ang shook her head. "Well, you certainly *look* homeless," she said. His face was dirty, and a wig made his hair long and stringy. He looked ten years older and twenty pounds heavier. "You're definitely unrecognizable."

"Okay," Sanderson said. "Let's get you wired up."

"Glad we're taking your car," Ang said to him, as they headed downtown.

Sanderson grimaced. "It'll take me a damn month to get the smell out."

"Um, guys, I'm the one who actually has to wear this shit all night," Hoyt said from the backseat.

They all grew quiet as Sanderson steered into one of the seedier parts of town. "Good luck," he said, as Hoyt got out of the car in the alley.

Hoyt nodded and disappeared into the dark shadows.

"He's still hurt," Ang said as they turned back onto the main road.

"He'll be fine. He knows what he's doing," Sanderson said.

Ang stared out the window.

Sanderson pulled into the RA's parking lot. "Go back to the hotel. Get some sleep. I'll bring him back."

"You better," she said.

After a long soak in the tub, Ang headed for Hoyt's room. Feeling tired, but wired and worried about him, she crawled under the covers of his bed. She breathed in deeply, lying on the pillow that smelled like him. It made her feel closer to him while she waited for him to come back to her.

HOYT STUMBLED down yet another back alley, keeping in the dark shadows. He smiled when he saw his informant in a small group crowded around a restaurant dumpster.

He approached with a slow shuffle.

When Paul looked up, Hoyt held out a bottle of cheap vodka. The guy took it and drank greedily. He wiped his mouth, then studied Hoyt for several minutes. "I know you," he said and cocked his head. "What's the opposite of 'you clean up well'?"

Hoyt had known the guy was sharp, but definitely hadn't expected to be recognized that quickly. "Figured I'd have better luck getting your friend to talk this way."

They walked away from the group, headed into the nearby park.

Paul shrugged. "He hasn't been around much lately."

"Where does he usually hang out?"

"Come with me." Paul nodded towards a more private area of the park.

He led the way to a bench at the end of a walking trail. The nearest light was burned out, leaving the area around them in nearly pitch black darkness.

They sat in silence, Paul drinking and Hoyt pretending to drink.

After twenty minutes, a slight figure in dark sweats, a hooded sweatshirt pulled over his head, slowly made their way down the path. The figure stopped and hesitated when he saw Hoyt.

"It's okay. He's a friend," Paul said softly.

The figure moved towards them.

Hoyt stood. "I'm John."

"Call me Edge," the man said, leaving the hood over his head.

"Tell him what you saw," Paul prompted.

Edge looked around, then focused on Hoyt. "I seen this guy in an alley. Right before the smoke. I knew her. The lady that died in the fire. We hang around the same area."

"The guy you saw," Hoyt said. "What did he look like."

The young man looked into Hoyt's eyes. "He looked like the fire chief."

"I believe you. So you hang around the area these fires have been happening?"

Edge nodded.

Hoyt slowly reached into his pocked. He handed Edge two hundred dollars and a cell phone. "This phone is clean. You see anything else, see if you can get pictures or a video. I'll make it worth your while."

Edge nodded, then started back down the path.

AT FOUR IN THE MORNING, Hoyt let himself into his hotel room.

He smiled when he saw Ang sleeping in his bed. He watched her for a full minute, before her nose wrinkled and she opened her eyes. "Hi," she said softly.

"Hi," he answered.

She sat up. "Did you get anything good?"

He nodded. "Let me shower, then I'll tell you all about it."

"God, yes," she said. "Then let's burn those clothes."

Hoyt spent a long time scrubbing himself in the shower. He wasn't one to take long leisurely showers, but it seemed liked it took forever to wash off the stench of his clothes and the underbelly of Casper. Worse, the information he'd found left him feeling tainted.

Ang had drifted back to sleep, but sat up as Hoyt exited the bathroom in a cloud of steam, running a towel over his shaved head. She smiled. "You look like you again."

He smiled, but it didn't reach his eyes.

"Come here," she said, lifting the edge of the covers.

He turned off the bathroom light, got into bed, then glanced at the clock and groaned. "We need to be at the RA in three hours."

Ang wrapped her arms around him, started massaging the knots in his shoulders. "Relax. I'll make sure we're there on time. You can fill us in then."

He sighed and relaxed as her hands worked their magic on him. His eyes drifted shut and he let go of all the tension and worry.

He was instantly awake when the alarm went off, pulling on his clothes even as Ang was just waking up and getting out of bed.

An hour later, they were in the car, with Ward driving, headed across town.

As soon as they walked into the RA, Hoyt immediately went to the coffee pot.

"I need to go back," he said after a few sips.

Ang wanted to argue, that he needed to wait a few days.

"Who's the guy that saw something?" Sanderson asked.

Hoyt shook his head. "I don't know. He calls himself Edge."

"Is this guy reliable?" Ward asked.

"Questionable," Hoyt admitted. "But he says he saw the fire chief and I believe him."

Ward knew enough about Hoyt's background to trust his judgement. "Okay," he agreed. "Let's keep an eye on our new fire district chief."

"Okay," Sanderson said. "Let's set up a schedule for surveillance on the fire chief." He turned towards Hoyt. "Let's give it a day or two, see if the guy contacts you. If not, try to make contact again."

Hoyt nodded. He knew it was the right call, but he would have gone back under right now if it meant solving the case.

. . .

AFTER HEARING NOTHING FROM EDGE, Hoyt threw himself into his undercover role over the next week, renting an old van to drive around town that wouldn't call attention to itself. He parked it in a public lot, kept his undercover clothes in a bag inside to quickly change into.

Men in power like the senator and the police and fire chiefs needed people to do their dirty work. If he could find those people, he was confident he could use them to bring an end to the corruption.

While Edge had been a no show, Paul turned up most nights. Hoyt couldn't deny the guy was growing on him. And he may well end up being the key to solving the case.

Hoyt tried to maintain a distance from Ang, but he was failing miserably. He was used to being in way worse conditions than under-cover as a homeless person in Casper, but he didn't want to bring anything dirty or unclean near Ang.

He was exhausted but couldn't stay away from her no matter how hard he tried. He knew he was being a little cold to her again, but he had to concentrate on work if they were both going to survive this case. He just didn't know if he would survive with his heart intact.

Gone were the almost cozy nights they'd shared.

They still spent most nights together, working late into the evening when he wasn't undercover, followed by intense love making. But they had very little conversation other than about the case. He should be relieved she wasn't pushing for more. But a big part of him wished she would. And how fucked up was that?

ANG KNEW Hoyt was holding things back from her again. It was like one step forward and two steps back with him. Most nights this week she'd woken up in the middle of the night alone and he'd been at the desk working on his laptop. If he wasn't undercover, he was up all night on the computer. Tonight was no exception. She sighed and pulled on her kimono.

Hoyt turned as she walked up behind him, then shut his laptop.

"What are you working on?" she asked.

"Nothing important, just go back to bed. I'll be there soon."

Ang studied his face. The new lines of fatigue around his eyes and his shorter hair made his face look even more harsh in the dim light. She just wished he would let her in, let her help him. She ached to touch him, bring him back to bed with her. "John. What aren't you telling me?" she asked softly.

God help him, he didn't want to lie to her. But better to tell a small lie now and have her safe than the alternative. "Nothing you need to worry about," he said.

"Hoyt-"

He cut her off with a finger on her lips. "Ang. Honey. I'm going to ask you to trust me."

"I'm your partner."

His eyes searched hers. "Please, Ang. Just trust me, okay?"

She knew she was probably making a mistake, but she couldn't say no to him. "Fine," she said. "Don't make me regret it." But she could feel the distance between them. He was pulling away from her. And she had no idea how to stop it. Or if she should even try.

Maybe it was better this way. They'd had a good time for a few weeks, but she knew it had to end sooner or later. She ignored the painful protest her heart made at the thought as she went back to bed alone.

HOYT OPENED his laptop back up after she left. The subtle scent of lavender hung in the air and he ached to follow her back to bed and curl up next to her warm body, make love to her, then sleep for a week.

God help him, he didn't know if he was strong enough to survive without her now.

When she and Ward found out he was holding things back from them again they'd both want to kick his ass.

Hell, maybe he could go back to work for Lash after they finished with him.

He forced himself to focus. None of that mattered now.

What mattered was ending this and making sure Ang made it home safely.

ANG WOKE up again and felt cold empty covers beside her. She rolled over and looked at the clock. Three in the morning and Hoyt still hadn't come to bed. She pushed her hair out of her face, got out of bed, and pulled her kimono back on.

Hoyt was still at his computer, head down on the desk, fast asleep. Her heart gave a little tug.

Ever vigilant, he woke up the instant she was at his side. He sat up, rubbed his eyes. Ang sat down on his lap, turned his laptop at an angle she could see.

He didn't argue, proving just how exhausted he was. Ang read what was up on the screen, a police report about a drug arrest from four months ago. She started scrolling through the file he had open, looking at more arrest records.

"The damn drugs again," she said.

"Yeah," Hoyt sighed.

Ang kept looking. "It's like the police make just enough arrests to look like they're fighting the war on drugs."

Hoyt yawned, unable to keep his eyes open.

Ang stood. "Why don't you get a few hours of sleep. I'll keep looking through these."

Hoyt sighed. "Okay, but wake me up if you find something."

Ang watched him stumble to the bedroom, then started a pot of coffee.

Three hours later, she thought she was onto something. She stood and stretched.

Then jumped when she felt a hand on her back. She glared up at Hoyt. Damn, he moved silently. It was unnerving.

She studied his face. He looked better. Still tired, but better.

He leaned against the desk, picked up her coffee cup and took a drink. "What did you find?" he asked.

She grinned. "Not as much as I'd hoped, but something."

"I'm going to order some real coffee instead of this in-room crap."

"Get some pancakes and bacon, too."

He nodded and picked up the phone.

While they waited for room service, she went through what she'd found. "There's a pattern here. We need to cross-reference the arrests with when your informants said there were drug shipments coming in. I think they're making arrests around the same time to take the focus off any drugs coming in."

"It could be something," Hoyt agreed. "We'll go over it with Sanderson and Ward."

They both turned at the sound of a knock on the door.

"But breakfast first," she said.

19

In the basement of his small cabin outside town, Ed marveled at the changes in his life. Just a few short months ago, he was mired in mediocrity with a job he liked, a wife he liked, and a life he generally liked. But something had been missing.

Excitement. Passion. Purpose.

Now, despite all the setbacks, he felt more alive than ever before. He looked down at the small bomb he'd just built. It was perfect. And it hadn't even been that hard to put together. A little research and it was amazing what you could find online.

He felt powerful, like he could do anything.

He hadn't managed to kill the FBI agents at the factory, but that was okay.

The senator was the weak link. He understood that now. The man had no control over his impulses. And he was the one the feds were looking at. Once he was gone, Ed would be free. He'd always be thankful to the senator for awakening his darker appetites, for helping him to see there was so much more possible in life than he'd ever considered.

But it was time for Ed to be on his own.

And he was more than ready.

.   .   .

THE NEXT MORNING, Ed watched the senator's apartment from a safe distance through his hunting binoculars. He hadn't been able to park close enough to watch from his car, but he had found an empty building across the street that he'd easily gained access to.

An hour earlier, just as dawn broke, he'd planted the small bomb underneath the senator's car. Now he had a front row seat for the show.

His heartbeat kicked up as he watched the senator leave his apartment building and head towards the car. The senator's driver held the door open for him. *This was it.*

Ed smiled as the senator bent to get in the car and he pushed the button on the remote control detonator.

What he didn't count on was the senator getting a phone call before he was all the way in the car. The senator put the phone to his ear and stood. The few steps he took away from the car as he talked saved his life.

The car exploded. There was a blinding flash of white light. The car was blown a foot in the air, the windows shattered and fiery pieces of metal and glass rained down onto the ground. Voices screamed and shouted from all directions.

Chaos erupted on the street.

Ed watched for another minute. Cursed when the senator slowly got up off the sidewalk. The damned bomb hadn't blown nearly as spectacularly as he'd hoped. *Shit.* He ran for his car.

HOYT AND ANG had been parked a block down the street, surveilling the senator.

"What the hell?" Hoyt said as the senator's car blew up in front of them.

They exited their car, pulled their guns in unison and ran towards the explosion.

"He's alive," Ang said, as they got closer and saw the senator who was down on the sidewalk, but moving, slowly getting to his feet.

Hoyt saw a figure running from the scene and followed.

He saw the man get into a car two blocks down. His instincts told him this man had planted the bomb. Why the hell else would he be running away from the scene?

The car the man got into was a blue late model sedan, but Hoyt wasn't close enough to get the license plate as it pulled away from the curb.

Hoyt ran after the car, pushing himself as hard as he could, ignoring the sharp pain and sticky wetness he felt underneath his shirt. He stopped, aimed his gun. He wanted to shoot, but he was too far away. And he didn't know beyond a shadow of a doubt the man in the car was guilty. The car accelerated around the corner. *Damn it to hell.* He bent over, trying to catch his breath, and held his side.

"You all right?" Ang asked, running up next to him a minute later.

Hoyt waved her off and started walking back down the street.

She sighed and watched him walk away, blending in with the crowd.

When Ang got back to the scene, Sanderson and the cops were all over the place, but there was no sign of her partner.

"Hoyt?" Sanderson asked.

She gave an annoyed shrug.

Sanderson shook his head. They'd deal with the man later. Now, they had work to do. "We're gathering witnesses. You want to start interviewing them?"

She nodded and headed for the crowd. She could see the senator in front of a TV camera, looking defiant with his suit disheveled and blood smeared on his forehead. No doubt he'd find a way to use this to his advantage.

ED CURSED the FBI agents again as he drove away from the scene. Taking a deep breath, he forced himself to drive the speed limit. He'd thought for a minute the FBI guy was going to get close enough to get him or disable the car. He took another deep slow breath, willing his heart rate to slow. For the first time, he seriously thought about surrendering. Today had been too goddamn close. But the thought of jail stopped him. No way could he get out of this without serving time. Not now.

But he could run. He could find a way.

He had to.

He was adaptable. Running wasn't failure. It was a new opportunity.

SINCE HOYT WAS STILL MIA after the bombing, Ang went by herself back to the RA. She met with Agent Sanderson again. Ward was already there, having spent the morning working at the RA looking at the pattern of drug arrests for the last few years. They talked through the morning's events as the news replayed video of the explosion. They'd managed to collect a decent amount of videos from traffic cams and store security. In addition, they'd found numerous witnesses with videos on their cell phones. It was a blessing and a curse that everyone was addicted to their phone.

"Anything from Hoyt?" Sanderson asked.

She shook her head. He still hadn't responded to her calls or texts. The urge to defend him warred with her anger at how he'd just up and disappeared. It wasn't like him to leave a scene like that. Unless he was really hurt. Or going off on his own. Again.

"What kind of car was it that Hoyt chased after?" Agent Sanderson asked.

She shook her head to clear the unpleasant thoughts. "I didn't get close enough, but I think it was a blue Ford Taurus, older model."

"Ok. I'll check it against what's registered to Ed Newkirk. See if we get a possible match. He's the only suspect we have that might have the knowledge to build a bomb."

He paused. "And have Agent Hoyt get in contact with me ASAP. We need to get his statement."

"I will," she said, wishing she knew where the hell Hoyt had gone.

Sanderson watched her leave. He understood Agent Hoyt's cowboy antics more than most. He just hoped the man didn't get himself killed or lose the best thing that ever happened to him. He glanced at Ward, who just scowled and shook his head, clearly frustrated with his missing agent.

ANG FINISHED the paperwork at the RA then went back to the hotel looking for Hoyt. She was still angry that he'd just left the scene without her but couldn't deny she was concerned about him. She pounded on his door but got no answer. She twisted the handle and found it open.

She stood in the living room, but there was no sign of him. "Hoyt!" she called out.

"In here."

She followed his voice to the bathroom. He was standing at the sink, shirt off, a needle in his hand. Her gaze fell to the bloody washcloth in the sink. "What in the hell are you doing?"

"I pulled some stitches chasing after the car."

"So you decided to just sew yourself back up?" she asked incredulously.

"Didn't feel like going back to the hospital." He gritted his teeth as he plunged the needle into his side.

"Jesus," she muttered, turning away.

"At least let me help you bandage it back up," she said, and stepped forward after he'd finished and started cleaning off the wound. "Does it hurt?"

"Hell, yes."

She shook her head. "You're crazy."

He reached down and raised her chin so he could look into her eyes. "I'm crazy about you." He hadn't planned on admitting it to her, but the pain had dulled his brain, allowing the truth to come out.

She turned her cheek into his palm. "You've been so distant these last few days, I . . ."

He cut her off with a finger against her lips. "Sometimes I have to be. It's the way I work best. I want you safe."

"Hoyt, we've been over this. This is my job. It's dangerous sometimes, but I knew that going in."

"That doesn't keep me from worrying. I didn't plan on caring so much."

"Well, God, I'm sorry you don't want to care about me, but you're stuck with me until this is over."

He was tired of holding back, tired of pretending he didn't feel like he did. He was just so goddammed tired. Fuck it all, he was getting this out in the open. Now. And damn the consequences. "See, that's the problem. I care too much. In fact, I think I'm in love with you." He brushed the hair back from her face. "And, I think you're in love with me."

She couldn't respond. Couldn't breathe. This was not what she'd expected from him. Not now. His intensity overwhelmed her. She took a step back. "I . . . I need to think about this."

He smiled confidently as she backed out of the bathroom, nearly tripping over her own feet. She couldn't deny they were good together, in bed and out. But *love*?

Five minutes later, Ang leaned against the door to her room and closed her eyes. *Damn him!* She hadn't wanted this to happen. It was supposed to be just a fling. Sex was a great stress reliever on jobs like this. And that's all it was supposed to be. She'd let down her guard. She didn't need this level of complicated right now. And she knew him well enough to understand how hard this was for him and she also knew he never said anything he didn't mean.

So now what?

She didn't even know what love was. Her father was her greatest hero and role model. But he'd hardly been the best example of a husband. He'd been devoted to her and her mother, yes, but he'd been more devoted to his country and his career. It didn't make him a bad person, just not the husband her mother had needed. They'd divorced when she'd been thirteen.

She didn't have many close friends and those she did have were either single or unhappily coupled. She'd certainly never come close to love in any of her failed attempts at a relationship.

What she and Hoyt had shared the past few weeks had been

amazing. Then he had to throw the L word out there like a bomb. She sure as hell wasn't going to tell him that her dad already had them married off. And how the hell could she even consider a real relationship right now in the middle of a case that was not only life or death but make or break for her career?

She wished she could ignore what was in her heart. The truth. She *was* falling in love with him, she couldn't deny it. He was a hard man, but he'd allowed her a glimpse of tenderness underneath that few people ever got a chance to see. He was an original, but was he capable of a real, committed relationship?

Was she?

She forced herself to start getting ready for bed.

There was no denying they made a good team, when Hoyt wasn't going off on his own, anyway. She'd always been the one in control in her past relationships. This time she felt totally off-balance. It was like the balance of power had shifted and now he was in control. She didn't like the feeling. The cocky son of a bitch.

She punched her pillow, knowing sleep would elude her.

THE NEXT DAY Hoyt made no mention of the conversation at all. There was no in-between with him. She either wanted to kiss him or smack him upside the head. She wondered what it would be like to be in a relationship with him when they weren't working a case together. What would it be like to spend days off with him?

They'd probably just drive each other crazy.

And she'd drive herself crazy thinking like this. They had to finish the case, that was the bottom line. Whatever did or did not happen between them would have to come second.

HOYT KNEW his confession had thrown Ang for a loop. He enjoyed seeing her off balance. But it was time to focus now. He should feel guilty for holding back details of the case from her. He'd finally made contact with Edge and had been working him hard. And the guy was responding well, scoping out areas similar to where the other murders had occurred.

He ignored the guilt of not sharing everything with Ang.

He would end this. And hopefully, Ward and Ang would both understand. Hopefully he'd still have a job. And if he had somehow earned any favors with the man upstairs, he'd have a chance at a normal relationship with Ang. He knew it was asking a hell of a lot, but his first priority had to be putting an end to this case. Anything else was just a bonus.

And at least if anything did happen to him, he'd told Ang how he felt about her.

He knew just how evil these bastards were. He wanted Ang as far away from them as possible.

He wanted to rip them apart, limb from limb. And he'd feel no remorse about it.

20

H oyt could tell something had happened as soon as he and Ang walked into Agent Sanderson's office. The agent in charge was talking animatedly on the phone, running a hand through his hair, causing it to stick out in all directions.

Sanderson hung up, turned to them. "They found the senator's missing security guy. Or what's left of him anyway. Guy that owns a junk yard on the edge of town noticed a nasty smell when he was walking the grounds with his dogs. Found the body in a trunk of one of his cars."

"Jesus," Ang muttered.

"How was he killed?" Hoyt asked.

"Not sure yet. We can run out there now."

"Let's go," Hoyt said, headed for the door.

Ang got into the back seat of Sanderson's car while Hoyt took shotgun.

Sanderson shot a quick glance at the rear view mirror, then at Hoyt, eyebrows raised.

Hoyt gave a subtle shake of his head. He did not want the other agent involved in their personal business any more than he already was.

Sanderson smiled and shook his head as he maneuvered the car through traffic.

A HALF HOUR LATER, they were all looking down at the decaying body of Tyler Coates, aka Buzz Cut, lying in the trunk of a rusted out white Buick Regal.

"Cause of death looks like a single gunshot wound to the forehead," Sanderson said, taking out his notebook.

Ang watched Hoyt, saw his jaw clench. She tried to read the emotions that crossed his face before he got them under control. *What the hell was going on with him now?*

He was holding something back from her. Again. He knew more about the dead man than he was letting on. She'd bet her career on it.

But of course he didn't say one word about it or what was going through his head. Not for the rest of the day. Or the night when they got back to the hotel and had dinner in the restaurant.

They rode the elevator up in silence to his floor.

He took her hand, pulled her inside his room and kissed her hard as soon as the door shut behind them.

She pulled back, breathing hard, trying to put some distance between them. "Want to tell me about the dead guy?"

"What do you mean?" Hoyt asked.

"Dammit, John. Tell me what you know."

He sighed. "You told me you trusted me."

"And I do, but this is my job, too. We're partners. Fifty-fifty, remember? I can't do *my* job if you're holding information back from me."

He took a step closer. "Ang," he said, putting a hand behind her head, rubbing the back of her neck. His warm breath and the heat of his body almost made her forget why she was mad at him. Almost.

She pushed against his chest, her fingers wanting to linger over the hard muscles under his shirt. "Stop it. I'm trying to have a serious conversation here."

He grinned at her, trailed a hand down to her hip, and pulled her close against his body. "I know you're ready for me. I can smell you."

And Ang could feel the wetness between her thighs. And the hardness of his erection pressed against her core. He was right, she ached for him. No other man had ever had this effect on her. But she wasn't going to give in, no matter what her traitorous body wanted.

She shook her head. Took a step back. "Talk to me. Please."

He reached for her again but didn't say a word.

She forced herself to take another step back, away from him, despite how much she ached for him. "You're not getting off that easy. Not this time."

He still didn't talk, so she forced herself to turn and leave the room, letting the door slam shut behind her. She'd given him the chance to talk to her and he hadn't. Not one damned word. She refused to think about how much that hurt. She couldn't. But she also couldn't be with someone who didn't trust her one hundred percent. That wasn't a true partnership. That wasn't love.

HOYT STARED at the closed door of his room. He ached to go after her. And not just with his dick. His entire being ached for her, including his heart.

He fought down the guilt. She'd been nothing but a loyal partner to him from day one.

But he didn't go, even knowing that he'd probably just lost her for good.

He clenched his jaw. He was going to end this. Ang was pissed about being left out, no question about it. Probably pissed enough to not want anything else to do with him ever again. But at least she'd be alive.

Ward wouldn't be happy either. But he'd deal with the ramifications to his career after Senator Westmoreland and Edmund Newkirk were behind bars.

He was going back out undercover tonight. Maybe he'd find out something useful that would help him end this.

. . .

PAUL SEEMED AGITATED TONIGHT. He calmed down a bit after a few long drinks of vodka from his paper wrapped bottle.

"What's going on?" Hoyt asked softly.

His informant just shook his head and started to walk away. Hoyt followed him as he walked down the street and turned into a dark alley.

Paul looked left and right. "I found someone who might have information that you can use."

"And?" Hoyt prompted.

Paul took another long drink. "And he's bad news. He's a big time dealer. Coke. Meth. Anything he can sell. But he agreed to talk to you about the senator. For a price."

"A price?"

"I sort of told him you'd pay him well for information."

Hoyt ran a hand down his face. "How much?"

Paul shrugged, took another drink.

"How. Much."

"The sum of five g's may have been mentioned."

Hoyt paced a few steps away, then turned back. "Jesus, fuck, Paul. I don't exactly carry that kind of cash with me undercover. And he's expecting this tonight?"

"I knew how important the information was to you. I saw an opportunity and made it happen." He shrugged, took another drink.

Paul's cell phone buzzed. "He's on the way," he said.

Five minutes later, Hoyt heard footsteps and turned to see a tall, stocky man in a dark hooded sweatshirt turn into the alley.

The guy nodded at Paul, then turned towards Hoyt. "You the fed with the money?" he asked.

Hoyt tried to not glare at Paul. Nothing like having his cover blown in a big fucking way. "What do you have?" he asked.

"Where's the money?"

"It's here." Hoyt stepped closer and stared hard at the punk dealer. "Make it worth my time."

"Okay. Look, I'm taking a hell of a chance coming here." He handed Hoyt a cell phone. "I've got recordings on here of the police chief. He made an arrangement with me to sell the drugs. He mentioned how he was protected. Not the senator by name, but he inferred it."

"Good," Hoyt said.

"There's more, but I need protection. If it gets out that I talked, I'm fucked."

"We can arrange that," Hoyt said.

The back of Hoyt's neck started itching. "Anyone know you're here?" he whispered.

The dealer shook his head.

Hoyt heard footsteps at the end of the alley. "We're about to have company."

Paul took a drink from his bottle.

The dealer pulled out another phone, started texting. "My guys are close. They're on the way."

"Any idea what we're facing?" Hoyt asked.

"Probably Max and his boys. A rival dealer. If it is and they followed me, it's going to get bloody."

Three men rounded one corner of the alley. Two more headed towards them from the opposite direction. All armed.

Hoyt had his gun hidden under his jacket, but wanted to avoid using it if possible.

But damn, this was about to get messy.

The five men converged on them.

Hoyt ignored the dealer and Paul, concentrated on the two men headed towards him.

Out of the corner of his eye, Hoyt saw Paul get in a good punch, knocking one of them out. Paul turned to Hoyt with a grin. The guy was willing to fight hard, but he was drunk. How much help was he going to be?

Paul never saw the knife coming towards him from the second man.

Hoyt moved forward, kicking the knife out of the guy's hand. He had a second to register Paul falling to the ground, then had to focus his attention on the other two men coming at him.

He heard a gunshot, heard the dealer they'd met grunt as he fell to the ground.

Hoyt couldn't do anything to help at the moment. He was surrounded by three of them now as the one who'd shot the dealer focused his attention on Hoyt. At least he had the element of surprise. They certainly didn't expect a homeless guy to be able to kick their ass.

He deflected most of the blows, landing more than he received. He kept going, kept fighting until he was the only one left standing.

He was pretty sure one of the guys wasn't going to get up ever again. He hadn't intended to kill anyone, but the guy was all jacked up on something, wouldn't stop coming at him.

Once he realized the immediate threat was gone, he made sure the dealer's phone was still in his pocket, then turned towards Paul, still sprawled on the ground. Not moving. *Shit.*

Hoyt dropped to his knees, assessed the wound, and balled up his jacket to try and stop the bleeding. He heard sirens in the distance, saw a few people on the street gawking and talking on cell phones. *Fuck.* He discreetly pulled out his phone, sent a 911 text to Sanderson. He didn't carry his badge undercover, so chances were good he was headed to jail if the cops got there before Sanderson. But he wasn't about to leave and let his informant bleed out in the damned alley. He'd deal with whatever consequences he had to face.

"Just hold on," he muttered to Paul as he continued applying pressure to the deep wound in the other man's chest.

A cop car screeched to a halt at the end of the alley, two officers jumped out, guns drawn.

"Hands on your head!" one of them shouted.

Hoyt stood and complied. "This man needs help," he said.

The officer looked around at the other bodies on the ground. "And what about them?"

"They don't matter. They attacked us."

"Yeah," the officer said, stepping forward. "You want to tell me how one homeless guy caused all this damage?"

"Not really," Hoyt said.

The officer just glared and kept his gun aimed at Hoyt's chest.

ANG HAD JUST WASHED her face and changed into her pajamas when her cell phone rang. *Sanderson*. She answered immediately.

"Hoyt's in trouble. I'm on the way to pick you up."

"Got it," she said. She hung up and quickly changed clothes and pulled her hair up. There was no time to think about worst-case scenarios. She would not allow her mind to go there. She was waiting outside the front door of the hotel when Sanderson pulled up.

"What's going on?" she asked, buckling up as he sped away.

"Not sure. He sent an emergency text with an address. There's been chatter about a possible drug deal gone bad and bodies in an alley near there."

"Shit," Ang said.

"Yeah." Sanderson kept his eyes on the road as he sped around traffic.

"Ward?" she asked.

"At the office reviewing the feed from Hoyt's wire."

Neither spoke for the rest of the short drive across town. He parked at the curb and they jumped out, pulled their badges and pushed their way through the crowd. Relief flooded over Ang when she saw Hoyt standing next to another cop and a paramedic.

Sanderson flashed his badge at the first officer he saw. "We need to get everyone to stay back, get a perimeter going." He nodded towards where Hoyt stood, facing off with the other officer. "He's one of ours."

"We still need to take him in."

"No, you don't."

While Sanderson was arguing with the cop, Ang continued to

push her way into the alley towards Hoyt. Her eyes scanned the broken bodies on the ground and she shuddered.

Ang flashed her badge at the cop and moved towards Hoyt, saw the blood covering his shirt. "You okay?" she asked, ignoring the mean looking cop who'd lowered his gun, but was still glaring at Hoyt.

"Not mine," Hoyt said, looking a little shellshocked as Paul was loaded into the ambulance.

Sanderson moved towards them. "Press is here. We're going to have to let them take you in," he whispered to Hoyt.

Hoyt nodded. It fucking sucked, but he understood. He slipped the dealer's phone into Sanderson's pocket.

Sanderson stepped back and Hoyt let one of the officers cuff his hands behind his back. He didn't speak as he was put in the back of one of the police cars. He didn't know if either of the cops in the car were dirty, so the best idea was to not say a word to either of them. At least the jackass that got in his face wasn't one of the two.

He ignored the driver's questioning glance in the rearview mirror, rubbed his grimy face against his shoulder. What a fucking nightmare. He leaned his head back and closed his eyes.

It wouldn't be the first time he'd been in jail.

And that was somewhere he really didn't want his mind to go, so he shut down the memories.

He sat up and opened his eyes once the car was stopped outside the police station.

Inside the station, Sanderson was having a stand off with the police chief.

"You damn well need to tell me when you have someone undercover in my town!" The chief was red-faced, yelling at Sanderson.

Sanderson ignored him. He put a hand on Hoyt's arm, led him down the hall and out the back door of the station, then into the backseat of the waiting car. Ang was in the front passenger seat. She turned towards him, concern etched on her face.

He forced an exhausted smile, thankful he wouldn't be spending the night behind bars.

She gave him a searching look, but didn't smile back.

No one spoke for a good long time as Sanderson drove across town.

Eventually, Sanderson broke the silence. He looked at Hoyt in the rearview mirror. "We got your transmission and the phone is being looked at. Ward has people on it as we speak. Your UC days in Casper are over, but we got some good intel. We'll go over it tomorrow morning."

Hoyt nodded but didn't speak.

Sanderson dropped them off at one of the hotel's side entrances. Hoyt headed inside while Ang paused and spoke to Sanderson. She quickly joined Hoyt in the hall a couple minutes later and they took the stairs to his room. Hoyt shut the door, leaned back against it.

"Paul's in surgery. Two of the dealers are in the hospital. Two are in jail. One's dead," Ang said.

Hoyt nodded, eyes closed. Ang stepped forward, ran a hand down his dirty face, leaned her forehead against his chest. He ran a hand through her soft hair. "I stink," he said.

Her laughter vibrated against him, making him smile. "Then let's get you in the shower," she said

He didn't protest as she took his hand and led him into the bathroom. She started the shower, then helped him peel off the dirty clothes. "You're dirty now, too," he said.

She smacked his ass as he got into the shower, then she shed her clothes and stepped into the warm spray next to him. "Guess we'll just have to get clean together."

He gave her a tired smile.

Ang wanted to cry as she gently cleaned his cut and bruised knuckles and ran her hands over the new bruises on his body. He lifted her chin until she was looking into his tortured eyes. He bent down, aggressively claiming her lips.

She hung onto his shoulders, lifting her legs to wrap around his hips. He braced a hand on the shower wall, sliding deep inside her.

"Ang," he said, as he began to move.

She knew he'd gotten good information tonight, but hated the cost he'd had to pay. She let the tears fall as the water washed them away. She closed her eyes, felt Hoyt's breath against her ear as he thrust inside her. She felt her orgasm building and let herself get lost in the moment. *We can face reality tomorrow,* she thought as she felt Hoyt thrust a final time, coming just after she did.

They took turns washing each other off again. Five minutes later, they were in bed under the covers.

"Sanderson said he doesn't expect us in the office before noon tomorrow," she said softly.

Hoyt shook his head. "There's too much to do. We're too close to take the morning off."

"Okay," she said, wrapping an arm around his chest.

He had to be hurting. She gently ran a hand over the bandage on his side.

Hoyt rolled over, propped himself up on an elbow. "You don't have to be gentle, and I'm more than up for round two," he said.

Ang smiled. She knew he didn't need to hear how much she worried about him. He'd taken down five armed drug dealers without firing a shot. He was more than capable of taking care of himself. But that didn't mean she liked seeing the damage to his body.

He cupped her face. "Look, I'm exhausted, I'm a little beat up, but trust me when I say this is nothing compared to what I went through in the SEALs."

"Well, okay, then, tough guy," she said, sliding her hand down lower on his body. "Let's get to round two then."

Afterwards, she felt his body relax, succumbing to the exhaustion she knew he had to be feeling. She closed her eyes, breathing in the scent of his warm, clean skin. She felt too keyed up about the night's events to sleep, but didn't want to risk waking him up. So she snuggled closer and let the silent tears fall.

When her alarm jarred her awake the next morning, she saw that Hoyt was already up, drinking a cup of coffee. She shook her head. The man was a machine.

Ang offered to drive to the RA, but he just raised an eyebrow and took the keys.

She shrugged and followed him out to the car.

SANDERSON STUDIED Hoyt as he and Ang walked into his office promptly at eight a.m. Other than a bruise on his jaw, battered knuckles, and a slightly stiff gait, Hoyt looked none the worse for the wear after his evening adventure. "Guess your time as a homeless man is up," he said.

"Thank God," Hoyt answered. "I couldn't stand the smell of myself."

"The even better news is, I was able to get the editor of the local paper to put a positive spin on last night's event. The headline should read something to the effect of 'armed drug dealers go up against two homeless Army vets and get their asses kicked'."

He didn't add that he and the editor had had a brief affair a year ago. It had ended amicably, both being too focused on their careers for a long term relationship. But they had maintained a productive working relationship and somewhat of a friendship.

"Anything on the dealer's phone yet?" Hoyt asked.

"Not yet, IT's working on it now. And on another note, the senator's wife has apparently flown back to their home in D.C. No idea if it's related to anything happening now, but it's worth noting."

"So what now?" Hoyt asked.

"Let's step up the pressure on the senator's aide. If we can get him to make a deal, wear a wire . . ."

"He knows what we look like. We'll go to overt surveillance on him," Hoyt said. "Step up the pressure in an obvious way."

"Sounds good. Start by following him home from work. Follow him in the morning. Stay on his ass," Sanderson said. "I'll rotate my people in when you need a break. And Cheyenne's sending a couple agents up in the morning. We'll put them on the senator."

.   .   .

SEAN ALSTON CONSIDERED himself to be a smart man. He'd worked damned hard to get where he was. He knew his boss was into all kinds of illegal activities. The man was brilliant, no question about it, but he was also a criminal. Sean could see the writing on the wall. The FBI was closing in. Hell, Sean hadn't gone anywhere the past two days without them following him everywhere he went.

He knew about the fire at the factory and the near death of the two federal agents. He could see the senator's mental state deteriorating. He could feel the noose tightening around his own neck and was smart enough that he knew he needed to bail while he still could.

He looked at the clock above his fireplace. It was time for him to leave for work. He looked out the front window. Yep, the car with the two agents was parked just down the street from his house again.

He swallowed hard. No time like the present.

HOYT SAT up straighter in the front seat of the car. "He's coming out the front door." He paused as they watched Alston cross the street, headed right for their car. "What the hell is he up to?" Hoyt asked as he rolled down the window and put his hand near his gun.

Alston stopped, looking suddenly nervous now that he was face to face with the two agents. He looked down at the ground, then up at Hoyt. "I want to make a deal," he said quietly.

Hoyt's first thought was to tell him to go fuck himself. *Now* the guy wanted to talk? But they needed information, and they needed it yesterday.

"Put me in witness protection, I don't care. But I'm damned well not going to jail," Alston continued.

Hoyt nodded. "Okay. Go to work like normal. Leave your back door open. We'll meet you back here tonight. We'll need anything you have, then we'll get you set up with a wire. Go from there."

Alston nodded, looked up and down the street, then headed back to his house.

"He's not exactly stealthy," Hoyt remarked.

"The asshole just wants to save himself," Ang bit out.

"Yeah, I agree, but we can use that," Hoyt said.

"And he gets to live out the rest of his life in cushy witness protection when he should be in jail."

Hoyt tried to hide how much her pissed-off side turned him on. "It's worth the trade off."

She sulked. "I know. It just sucks."

"It does," he agreed.

"But if he can get us enough for a warrant, and we get the senator, it will be worth it," she said.

"That's the spirit," Hoyt said, leaning over to give her a quick kiss.

SEAN LET himself into his house at 5:25 that evening. He sighed and rubbed the back of his neck, then jerked to attention when he felt someone watching him from the living room.

Hoyt and Ang had been sitting in the dark, waiting for him to get home. Hoyt smiled, enjoying the other man's discomfort.

"I know I said I'd leave the door unlocked, but damn, you could have said something."

Sean turned the light on and sat in the chair opposite where Hoyt and Ang sat on his couch. He leaned forward. "Look, I know what you guys probably think of me, but - "

Hoyt cut him off. "It doesn't matter. The only thing that matters is if you can get enough dirt on the senator to put him away and save your own ass in the process."

"What do you need?"

"You'll need to wear a wire. Access his computer files if possible, get any paper records we can use," Hoyt said.

Sean gave a nervous laugh. "And here I thought you'd ask for something hard."

Ang shrugged. "Easier than going to prison."

"And if I do this? Then what? I go into protective custody?"

"We can arrange that," Hoyt said.

"Okay. Okay," Sean said, sounding like he was trying to convince himself.

Hoyt stood, pulled out a backpack. "We have everything you need here. We'll go over how everything works, that way we won't have to come back and risk being seen together." Hoyt started pulling equipment out of the bag.

Sean swallowed hard, his eyes darting around the room.

"Focus," Hoyt said. "Your life may very well depend on this."

Ang stood. "You look like you need a drink."

Sean turned to her. "I have a nice Laphroig scotch in the kitchen."

Ang disappeared then came back with three glasses of scotch on ice. She passed them out. "Let the Spy 101 continue."

By the time they left two hours later, Sean had a burner phone, instructions on how to copy files from the senator's computer, and a wire setup that they could listen in on.

"What do you think?" Ang asked as they drove back to the hotel.

Hoyt rubbed the back of his neck. "I don't know. It'll go one of two ways. He'll totally screw it up and get himself killed, or he'll bumble around and actually get something we can use."

Hoyt, Ang, Ward, and Sanderson gathered in the conference room at the RA early the next morning.

"You think the little shit can pull it off?" Ward asked, pouring a cup of coffee.

"Probably not," Hoyt said. "But right now, he's our best shot."

They finished setting up the listening equipment and went over the tasks for the day. They all stopped what they were doing when they heard a whispered voice.

"Hey. You guys hear me?"

Hoyt put in an earpiece. "We hear you."

"Okay. Good. I'm, uh, at work."

"We got you. Stop talking," Hoyt said.

The next sound they heard was a toilet flush.

"We're so fucked," Sanderson said.

. . .

THEY TOOK turns monitoring the wire feed and alternating surveillance with Sanderson's men and the agents from Cheyenne.

Two days later, they still had nothing. Hoyt stood and rolled his shoulders.

Sanderson looked at the clock. 5:05 on Friday night. Another wasted day. He started to take out his earpiece.

"Sean!" A shouted voice echoed. Sounded like the senator.

"Sir?" Sean asked.

"Why are you still here on a Friday night?"

"Just finishing up, sir."

"I wish everyone had your work ethic. I got to deal with damn police chiefs and fire chiefs that can't keep their people in line." There was a loud sniff. "Dumb fucking shits."

Ang cocked her head. "Jesus. Is he high?'

They listened to the senator ramble nonsense for a few more minutes before the sound of a door slam.

"He's gone. His office door's unlocked. I'm going to search inside," Sean whispered.

"Okay," Hoyt said. "Start with his desk."

"There's some white powder residue here. I think it's coke," Sean said as they heard shuffling papers and drawers being opened. "One of the drawers is locked."

"Look for a key taped underneath the desk," Hoyt said.

They could hear the sound of Sean's rapid breathing.

"Breathe, stay calm," Ang said.

"Okay, okay. I can't find a key."

"It's okay," Hoyt said. "Is the computer on?"

"It's on. He didn't lock it up!"

"Keep your voice down," Hoyt said. "Do you have the thumbdrive?"

"Yeah, plugging it in now."

"What files do you see?" Hoyt asked.

There was a pause, then a booming voice. "What the fuck are you doing in here?"

"I - "

"What are you doing to my computer?"

Hoyt turned to Sanderson. "Get whoever's closest in there now!"

Sanderson grabbed his phone. Before he could say a word, they all heard the sounds of a struggle. Then glass shattering followed by a scream and a thud. Then nothing.

"Did he just . . ?" Ang started.

"Oh, my God," Sanderson said, then started yelling into his phone. "Everyone get to the senator's office now."

Hoyt dialed 911 as they all ran outside and jumped into Sanderson's car.

Police Chief Delaney was on his way home when he heard the call. Details were still sketchy, but it sure as hell sounded like someone had taken a header from the senator's ninth floor office. Delaney seriously doubted it was the senator himself. The guy was crazy, but not suicidal.

He drove down a deserted road a few miles from his house. He parked and shut off the headlights. It had all started out so easy. Look the other way a few times, ignore a few crimes here and there. His wife had gotten suspicious about where all the new money they had was coming from. She'd taken off a month ago and wouldn't return his calls. But Delaney had continued to believe in the senator. And to enjoy the extra money. He supposed he'd enjoyed the thrill of what he was doing, too.

But now, it was all coming to a crashing halt. He knew it in his bones. He didn't see an easy way out for any of them now. It was over. And he was tired.

But he'd be damned if he was going to be put away in his own jail.

He pulled out his gun. He should have tried harder with his wife. Now all that money would just go to waste.

There was already an ambulance and several cop cars on the scene when Sanderson pulled up in front of the senator's office building. Sanderson led the way, Ward, Hoyt, and Ang right behind him.

"What do we have?" he asked the first cop they came to.

The cop nodded towards the top floor of the building. "Looks like the guy was thrown through the window."

Sanderson looked down at the body. He was barely recognizable, but it definitely looked like a very dead Sean Alston.

"My partner and one of your guys went upstairs to take a look," the cop continued.

"Chief Delaney around?" Sanderson asked, wondering how the guy would react to this.

The cop shook his head. "We haven't been able to raise him."

Sanderson and Hoyt exchanged a look.

Ward nodded to Sanderson. "Let's head up to the senator's office." He turned to Hoyt and Ang. "See what you guys can find out here. I'll get someone to watch the senator's house in case he heads home."

"That was definitely the senator's voice we heard," Ang said as they approached the body.

Hoyt was kicking himself for not being able to stop the senator sooner. Now another person was dead. "How did we not realize how unstable and twisted he is?"

Ang could see the anguish in his eyes. "Sean made the decisions that put him in the place he was in. This is *not* your fault."

Hoyt ran a hand down his face. "I know that. There are just too many dead bodies left in the wake of this. And two of the main players are MIA."

While Ang talked to the cops and witnesses, Hoyt stepped aside to assess the scene. The senator and police chief were nowhere to be found. Where was the fire chief? His gut told him they needed to find the guy.

He had the keys to the bureau car in his pocket. He glanced at Ang, who was facing way from him, then nodded to the cop next to him. "I need to get back to the office. Can you give me a quick lift?"

He didn't go into the RA when he got there, instead taking one of bureau cars back to the hotel. He spent the next hour calling every informant he had the number for. He'd pay everything in his bank account personally if one of them came up with the location of the fire chief.

He ignored the messages Ang and Sanderson left for him, knowing they'd both be tied up at the scene for a good long while.

21

E d drove down the long rutted gravel road to his cabin. His wife had already gone to bed at nine when he'd left the house. He didn't leave a note, didn't take anything with him. Just walked out the front door.

As he was leaving, his phone rang. It was the senator. Ed ignored the call.

And damn, it had felt liberating. The moon shone bright, illuminating the road, as if just for him and he knew he was on the right path.

They'd had some good years, he and his wife, but he didn't think he'd even miss her. It wasn't like he hadn't loved her, more like she'd served her purpose. And now it was time for him to move on.

The fire station would be in for a surprise the next morning when he didn't show up for work. He chuckled. Like his wife, the job had served it's purpose. He'd given it so many years of his life, but he was ready to move on.

He was going to run. He'd taken out all the money he could get his hands on, even sold his wedding ring. It wasn't enough, but he'd make do. He'd adapt.

He had some emergency supplies stored at the cabin. He'd

destroy the evidence from the fires he'd set, get some sleep, gather up his supplies, then hit the road.

He felt powerful enough now that he was actually looking forward to starting over somewhere new.

The possibilities were endless.

SENATOR WESTMORELAND CURSED as he hung up the phone. How dare Ed not answer his call. The little shit. After everything he had done for the man. After all the sacrifices he'd made. He'd make the ungrateful son of a bitch pay, he vowed.

Right after he took care of those damned pesky FBI agents.

HOYT'S PHONE rang at one in the morning. It was Edge.

"Tell me you have something for me."

"I got something. Someone saw the fire chief at a pawn shop a few hours ago. I sent someone over to his house. They saw him pull out about a half hour ago. Headed north, out of town."

Ed's cabin was north of town. "You did good, Edge."

"So, I'll get the money."

"You'll get the money. You have my word."

Hoyt hung up and checked his weapon, refusing to think about how alone he felt. He knew Ed was going on the run. And he was going to stop him. He tried to remind himself that this was what he wanted, to end this on his own. That he was doing it for the right reasons.

The thought of food turned his stomach, so he downed a quick cup of coffee in the hotel lobby then drove out of town, following his instincts, following what he hoped would be the lead that would end this case.

He thought about calling Sanderson. But the guy was too by the book. He'd want to wait around for the search warrant. But by then, Ed would be long gone. And Hoyt would not accept that outcome.

And he sure as hell wasn't going to waste time waiting around for backup.

It wasn't that Hoyt didn't like to follow the rules. But when it came to Ang's safety, the rule book went right the fuck out the window.

As he pulled out of the motel parking lot, he refused to think about Ang any more. It hurt too damned much. He couldn't afford any distractions. Not now. Not when he was so close to ending this.

Hoyt wasn't in his room and he wasn't answering his phone. And Ang had a damned good idea what he was doing. He was shutting her out and trying to end this on his own. How could he tell her he loved her and then refuse to talk to her and pull a stunt like this? He wasn't healed yet and had no business going out on his own as if he had no regard for his own life.

As angry as she was, she was also worried about him. Which was stupid considering how he was treating her. But she was not going to let him go on a suicide mission.

She sighed. She needed to calm down. She needed to let Ward know what was going on. She picked up her phone.

"It's Agent Nobles," she said when her boss answered. "Hoyt took off on his own."

"Do you know where he went?"

"Not for sure."

Ward paused. "You can't stop him."

"Dammit, he's not back to a hundred percent yet. What in the hell is he thinking?" she asked, exasperated.

"He'll call for backup if he needs it, I know what you're thinking. Don't do it. Wait for Sanderson or I to get there."

"I have to go. I'm sorry."

"Shit!" Ward cursed as she ended the call. That's all he needed, two rogue agents running around. He shrugged into his coat as he called in backup. If they didn't get themselves or each other killed, he'd do it for them.

. . .

ANG HAD a hunch where Hoyt had gone; she'd seen it in his eyes when they'd been there before. Edmund Newkirk's hunting cabin outside of town. He was hurt and she was not going to let him do this on his own. Tough as he may be, he needed her help. He needed a partner. He was just too damned stubborn to admit it.

She sped out of town, hoping she was right about where he was headed. It was only a quarter after two. He couldn't have that much of a head start on her.

She spotted Hoyt's borrowed bureau car parked off the road about a half mile from the cabin. She parked behind it, then called Ward and gave him the location. She ignored his instructions to wait for backup and hung up.

She ran a hand down her face. She'd just hung up on her boss. No matter how this turned out, she'd be lucky if she still had a job when this was all over. And her dad would kill her anyway if she made it out of this alive.

But Hoyt was in there alone, possibly with a psychopathic murderer. She couldn't wait. She picked her way through the trees and approached the dark cabin, gun out.

She paused outside a small rundown garage. Ed's car was parked inside.

Her heart rate kicked up. This was it.

She checked her gun and headed through the darkness towards the cabin. The only sound was the wind whistling softly through the trees.

22

Hoyt made his way through the cabin in the dark, looking for something, anything they'd missed. It didn't *feel* abandoned, he felt a presence here, something just didn't add up.

The back of his neck was itchy.

He was good at picking up the most subtle of human vibrations and he'd felt them here in this house earlier, felt them now. Someone was in the house. He was not alone, he was sure of it. And he was going to finish this. He smiled a predatory grin. Time for the mother-fucker to pay.

There was more to the small cabin than first appeared. There had to be. He'd carefully searched each room. Found nothing. No one. No sign anyone had been there recently. He was missing something.

He closed his eyes, picturing the layout. A basement? That was the only thing that made sense.

He slipped off his shoes and methodically went through each room again.

He'd completed another full circuit of the house and still found nothing. Had he been wrong? He leaned against the counter in the kitchen, trying to figure out where he'd made a mistake.

His eyes scanned the room, stopping on the rug in the middle of the floor. It was slightly off center.

He stepped closer, smiling when he saw the outline of a trap door.

He silently lifted the door and crept down into the darkness.

ED HAD HEARD the subtle noises above him. Whomever was up there was being quiet, but Ed knew every creak and groan of this cabin. He was not alone. Someone was here. And he had a damned good idea who it was.

And *no one* was going to ruin his plans now. Not now. He was too close to getting away and starting a new life.

HOYT WAS in the middle of a dark hallway. There was a faint light underneath a door on the right. He silently headed towards it, his breathing steady, gun out and ready.

ED HAD HIDDEN in a closet halfway down the basement hall. Listening. He sprung out of the shadows when he heard the subtle movement coming towards him. He threw the door open, tackling Hoyt from behind.

The son of a bitch FBI agent was here and he was ruining everything. It was not acceptable. He was too close to freedom. He'd kill the son of a bitch with his bare hands. Then burn the cabin to the ground with the body inside.

Freedom was so fucking close he could taste it.

They crashed into a shelving unit along the wall and tumbled to the ground. Hoyt's gun flew out of his hand and skidded across the floor, out of reach.

Hoyt hadn't expected anyone to be hiding in the closet behind him. He shouldn't have underestimated his opponent.

Damn, the guy was strong, and big. Hoyt felt the full force of that weight pressing down against his throat, cutting off his air. He kicked and bucked, trying to throw him off, but the grip on his throat didn't lessen.

ANG EASED OPEN the front door of the cabin and immediately heard crashing from the back of the house. She raced towards the sound and ended up in a small kitchen. The noise had definitely come from this direction, but below. She couldn't risk calling out, didn't want whomever might be down there to be aware of her presence. Especially if it wasn't just Hoyt.

She scanned the room, letting her eyes adjust to the low light. There had to be a basement, but where the hell was the entrance? There was no visible door she could find. She couldn't risk turning on the lights. She ran her fingers along the wall, then the floor, looking for something, anything to get down there, to get to Hoyt.

She nearly tripped over the cast off rug in the dark kitchen and dropped to her knees, seeing the outline of the open trap door.

She moved silently down the stairs and into the darkness below.

HOYT'S VISION started going gray and every cell in his body was screaming for oxygen. His lungs burned. He could feel his body weakening. He reached out blindly, his fingertips brushed against something cold and smooth. And heavy. A wrench. Gathering the last of his strength, he gripped it and swung it up against Ed's head.

Ed groaned and released his grip just enough for Hoyt to throw him off. Hoyt struggled onto all fours and managed to gulp in a few desperate breaths before Ed recovered and kicked him in his bad side, sending him flat on his back again.

Hoyt ignored the blinding pain and kicked out, catching Ed in the knees and sending him crashing down to the floor next to him. Hoyt was on him in an instant, his fists flying, pounding with all the fury he had left inside.

It ended. Here and now. He ignored the pain in his hands, in his side. Ignored the panting of his labored breathing. Couldn't stop now.

. . .

ANG FOLLOWED THE DARK HALLWAY; she could hear the sounds of a struggle and peeked around the doorway. She could barely make out Hoyt and Ed rolling around on the floor, both reaching for a gun. Dammit, she couldn't get a clear shot, if Ed would move just a little to the left ... She took a deep breath, waited for the right moment. Then flipped the light switch.

She used the brief hesitation as they both blinked at the sudden brightness to take aim.

Hoyt heard the shot a second before the patch of red appeared on Ed's shoulder. Ed gazed in fury at the doorway, his face a mask of shock and rage. The pause was just enough for Hoyt to get him face down on the floor, hands behind his back, ignoring the other man's grunts of pain. He'd already snapped the cuffs on when Ang stepped into the room, gun at her side.

"What are you doing here?" he asked, his voice hoarse, breath ragged.

"Saving your ass."

"I had it under control."

Her eyes flashed. "You shouldn't have gone in by yourself."

The sounds of sirens wailing filled the air. "I called Ward. Something you should have done," she added.

"I didn't know if I'd find anything." He was bent over, hands on his knees, breathing hard.

"Bullshit." She ignored the sympathy she felt and glared at him as she walked past. Why did he have to be so goddamn stubborn? She ran a shaking hand through her hair. She'd been so afraid something had happened to him. Why the hell did she care so much?

The small basement was soon teeming with police and FBI agents, including their boss and Agent Sanderson. Ed was pulled off the floor and taken into custody. It was all a blur.

"You two wait for me outside," Ward's stern voice commanded.

She watched Hoyt's jaw clench as he left the room. *What the hell was going on with him now?*

Sanderson shot her a sympathetic look and shrugged.

She smiled back, then followed Hoyt outside. Sanderson really was a nice guy. Why the hell couldn't she be attracted to someone like him?

HOYT MADE it outside and onto the porch before his legs gave out. He sank down on the front steps, suddenly exhausted. Too goddamn close for comfort.

He heard footsteps, then Ang sat down beside him, handed him his shoes.

She stared out at the road, barely visible in the pre-dawn light, trying to get her anger under control, then turned to face him. She could just make out the raised red marks on his neck and her anger faded to concern. "Are you hurt?"

"I'm fine," he said, voice hoarse.

"Your side?"

"I said I'm fine."

"You don't look fine."

"Goddammit, I said . . ."

They both jumped to their feet at the sound of Ward's footsteps behind them. "Over here," he said gruffly, walking around the side of the house.

They followed him in silence.

Ward glared from one of them to the other. "I should fire both of your asses right now." He looked Hoyt up and down. "You could have gotten yourself killed going in there alone like that. You know better than that. You're part of a team and you damn well better start acting like it."

"And you," he turned to Agent Nobles, "I don't care what your personal feelings are, you still have to follow procedure.

"I could very well be looking at two body bags on their way to the morgue right now." He looked up at the sky. "Thank God, I'm not." He paused, letting his words sink in. "Believe me, I know how hard it is, and I've stepped outside the line myself a few times, but this is not how we handle a case." He looked them each in the eye, his gaze steady. "You are quite possibly two of the best agents I've ever come across and it would be a shame for you to end up dead because you let your emotions control you. Lecture over. No more crazy stunts, okay?"

"Okay," they answered in unison.

Ward looked at Hoyt's neck and put a hand on his shoulder. "Now let's get you checked out."

"I'm fine, sir."

Ward's gaze drifted down to where Hoyt was holding his side. He raised an eyebrow and Hoyt let his hand drop.

"Maybe so, but I'm not taking any chances, so get your ass in the damned ambulance. That's an order."

Hoyt clenched his jaw, but headed to the waiting ambulance.

Ang watched him walk away without another word to her. She considered going back to the motel, packing, and getting the hell out of there. But she couldn't bring herself to do that. Not with the unfinished business between them.

She turned back towards her boss. "What about the senator?" Ang asked.

Ward smiled. "Ed has already started spilling his guts. It won't be long until he's picked up. And the guys from Cheyenne are still going through his office."

"Good," Ang said.

"I'll clean up here. You can head back to the hotel." He paused. "Or the hospital."

Ang stared down the driveway. Not for the first time in her life, she felt like she was at a crossroad that could significantly alter the path she was on.

FIVE MINUTES LATER, Ward stood in the basement watching his agents go over the crime scene. *God, those two were good.* He'd held back a lot out there. Hoyt's instincts may very well be better than his own. Once he learned how the system worked, he'd be unstoppable. And Agent

Nobles, *Jesus, what a shot!* She was every bit as good as her father. Maybe better. He shook his head. They made quite a pair.

The police chief's body had been found near near his home, dead of an apparent self-inflicted bullet wound. They had a manhunt underway for Senator Westmoreland. It was only a matter of time and they could all go home.

23

The last damned place Hoyt wanted to be at the moment was the hospital. But he tried his best to be patient as the doctor completed his exam.

"Nice job on the stitches," the doctor said, putting a new bandage on Hoyt's side.

Hoyt grunted in response.

The doctor looked at him over his glasses. "Your neck will be bruised and sore for a while, but there's no deep damage or swelling, so you're free to go."

Hoyt pulled his shirt back on as soon as the doctor left the exam room. The case was all but over. It was time to go back home. Not that he had much of a home to go back to.

He sighed wearily, feeling a bone deep exhaustion. He knew he'd fucked up. And he wouldn't blame Ang if she hated him. Hell, she was probably long gone, requested a transfer, and he'd never see her again.

The thought of never seeing her again cut so deep he wanted to double over in pain. He fought to keep his breathing even. He forced air in and out of his lungs.

Jesus, how could one tiny little woman have this kind of power over him?

He'd have to track her down. Make her understand.

He was sure groveling would be involved. But he'd happily do it. He'd do whatever it took to keep her in his life, he resolved as he pushed open the door.

ANG WAS WAITING in the hallway when Hoyt came out of the examining room. The sight of her standing there looking disheveled but utterly beautiful nearly brought him to his knees.

"I didn't think you'd be here," he said.

"You were hoping," she said with a slight smile.

"Maybe."

Her smile faded as her eyes swept down to the marks encircling his neck, already turning a deep purple. He watched her shudder. "Hey," he said, tilting her head up so their eyes met. "I'm fine." He smiled. "And we did it. We got the evidence. We got Newkirk. And the senator won't get far."

She nodded and smiled, but it didn't reach her eyes. He searched his exhausted brain for something to say that would fix things with her, came up with nothing.

They walked in silence to the car. As she was putting the key in the lock with a trembling hand, he reached out and grabbed her arm, spinning her around to face him. "Look, I'm sorry about what I said and about not telling you what I was doing. I just, I was scared," he admitted, looking at her hard. "And I was mad at myself for letting emotion cloud my judgment."

She looked down. "Hoyt, it's okay."

"No, let me finish. I wanted to keep you safe, but you definitely proved you could handle yourself. You're good at what you do and I was wrong to try and keep you from doing it."

His words touched her. She looked steadily at him for a moment. "Don't shut me out again."

"I won't."

"I mean it. I don't want to be shut out of your life, professional or personal. I want all or nothing."

"You may regret saying that," he replied as his lips quirked.

"Probably," she agreed.

His smile broadened. He'd never needed anyone before, but my God, he needed her. "I may have to make an honest woman out of you, though."

She arched an eyebrow at him. "John Hoyt, are you trying to propose to me?"

"I'm trying." God knows, that wasn't what he'd intended to do today, but if he had the chance to make her his forever, he was damned well going to take it.

Her eyes widened. She threw her arms around his neck and pressed her lips against his.

He pulled back, cocked his head. "Is that a yes?"

"Yes, yes yes!"

"Good." He pulled her close again, loving the feel of her body melting into his, where she belonged. "Then let's go home."

SENATOR WESTMORELAND WATCHED the two FBI agents embrace from a safe distance in the early morning light. How touching. He'd always appreciated a good love story. Too bad the agents wouldn't get their happily ever after. It was time for their fairy tale to end.

The drugs in his system made him feel invincible.

Ed would take the fall for the fires. And they'd never find enough evidence on his other activities. He'd just have to find another outlet for his passions.

Once this last loose end was tied up.

He loaded the gun and shook his head as he focused on what needed to be done. Some things you just had to take care of yourself.

A SLIGHT MOVEMENT in Hoyt's peripheral vision had him turning towards the trees at the edge of the hospital parking lot. His mind instantly cataloged the flash he saw. Gun.

He pivoted and pushed Ang to the pavement, felt the searing hot pain in his back as he threw his body down over hers.

Ang gasped, trying to get air into her lungs. She felt deja vu as Hoyt's weight pressed on top of her again. "John? What the hell happened?"

He grunted, struggled to roll off her. "Shooter. Trees."

She moved to a crouch next to him, automatically pulling her own gun. Her eyes scanned their surroundings.

Hoyt hadn't moved and her gaze fell to the blood on the front of his shirt. "Dammit, John," she said, focusing on the wound.

"Through the back, exit out the shoulder muscle," he said, voice tight. "I'll be okay."

Her gaze darted to the hospital then down to the rapidly spreading pool of blood underneath Hoyt.

"Go. Get him," Hoyt said through clenched teeth.

She nodded and ran towards the trees.

Hoyt cursed as he watched her take off. He wanted to be with her, to keep her safe. But he had to trust her and her abilities. So he let his head drop back down to the hard ground as he heard people shouting around him and waited for the paramedics to take him back into the damned hospital.

ANG RAN, trying not to think about Hoyt bleeding on the pavement behind her. She had to catch the guy who'd shot him. And she had a damned good idea who that was.

She recognized the senator as she got closer. He was dressed in jeans and a tan sweatshirt, but she knew it was him.

"Westmoreland," she yelled. "Stop, or I *will* shoot."

He kept running and Ang cursed. She'd almost caught up to him when he tripped over a fallen branch and went to his knees, breathing hard.

She approached cautiously. "Turn around and put your hands up," she commanded, stepping closer.

He stood and glared at her. "You do know who I am, right?"

"Oh, I'm very aware of who you are and what you've done, senator." She kept her gun aimed at his center of mass. "Hands on your head. Now."

He smiled. "You sure you want to do this, little girl? I'm sure we can come to some sort of *arrangement*." His smiled turned predatory.

Jesus, the guy had to be insane. "Not a fucking chance in hell," she said, moving her finger to the trigger. "This is your last chance. Hands on your head now, or I *will* shoot."

He cocked his head as the sound of sirens carried towards them. He started to take a step back, but must have seen the deadly intention in her eyes. He slowly raised his hands above his head. "You win this round," he said. "But it's not over."

"It is over," she said, as she stepped forward, reached into his jacket pocket and retrieved his gun, then cuffed his hands behind his back.

She kept her gun out, marching him back to the hospital parking lot.

"I got your boyfriend though. Got him real good. Maybe he'll even die," the senator said as they walked.

Ang would not let the words get to her no matter how much they cut through her. "He's fine," she said, hoping like hell it was true. "Keep moving."

"WELL, this has to be a record for the shortest time between visits I've ever seen," the doctor who'd treated Hoyt less than an hour ago said as they wheeled him in to surgery. "Three visits in less than a week. I hope you've got good insurance."

"Lucky me," Hoyt said, fighting the pain to stay conscious. He had to stay awake, had to make sure Ang was okay. He struggled to sit up. "Ang," he said.

"Lay back down. We need to get you into surgery."

"Not yet," Hoyt ground out. He needed to see Ang. Now. "This isn't my first go around with a bullet."

The doctor looked down at him. "Just because the bullet missed anything vital doesn't mean you're out of the woods. The longer we wait, the more blood you lose, the harder you make my job."

Damned if he didn't hate giving up control. But he had to trust the doctor, had to trust Ang. He closed his eyes.

"She'll be waiting for you when you wake up," the doctor said gently.

Hoyt sighed and let the darkness take him.

WARD HAD JUST GOTTEN BACK to his hotel room when his cell phone went off. He glanced down. It was Agent Sanderson's number. He sighed. The door had barely closed behind him. He looked longingly at the king sized bed across the room. He should have known his day wasn't over yet.

"I hope you're calling with good news," Ward said as he answered.

"I wish," the other agent said. "I just got a call about a shooting at the hospital parking lot. Details are sketchy, but I know Agent Hoyt was admitted back into the hospital, no word on Agent Nobles yet. I'm on my way there now."

Ward shook his head. *Goddamn.* Those two were going to be the death of him. He grabbed his car keys. "See you there," he said as he ran out the door and down the hall.

THE HOSPITAL PARKING lot was full of flashing lights when Ang marched the senator out of the woods. Six police officers and two of the local FBI agents immediately surrounded them.

Agent Sanderson jogged across the parking lot towards them.

"You okay?" he asked, his eyes darting from the senator to her.

She nodded. "I'm good."

She was more than happy to hand over Senator Westmoreland to him.

"This is all a mistake," the senator shouted. "None of you will have jobs after I'm done with you."

"How about you just shut the fuck up?" Sanderson said, roughly jerking him towards the nearest police car.

As soon as the senator was safely in custody, Ang ran towards the hospital.

She flashed her badge at the reception desk.

"John Hoyt, he was just brought in with a GSW. I need to find out how he is."

The bored looking red-haired woman barely looked up at her as she typed on her keyboard. "He was discharged this afternoon."

"Yes, I know. But he was brought back in." Ang knew she was being rude, but her nerves were shot. She kept seeing the spreading pool of blood on the pavement under Hoyt.

The receptionist looked back at her computer, then raised her eyebrow in surprise. "Ah, sorry, he's in surgery."

"Okay." Surgery wasn't too bad. He would be fine. It was just his shoulder. There was no need to panic. She took a deep breath, headed to the waiting room.

The adrenaline high was fading, leaving her feeling weak and shaky. She got a coffee and candy bar from the vending machine. The sugar and caffeine hit her bloodstream, making her feel more alert.

Had Hoyt really asked her to marry him? Had she really said yes?

Damned stubborn man, throwing himself in front of bullets to save her.

He'd be fine. He had to be. She would not accept the alternative.

Ever since she'd met him, she'd felt like she was on a roller coaster. She pictured his face as he'd asked her to marry him, the underlying vulnerability in his eyes. Her stomach contracted. She sure as hell wanted a chance to make a life with him.

ANG WAS PACING THE HALLS, still waiting for Hoyt to get out of surgery when Ward arrived.

The sight of her boss and his strong, calm presence reassured her.

"Can't leave you two alone for a minute," he said, shaking his head. "Where's Hoyt?"

She lifted her head, fighting sudden tears. "In surgery. He got hit in the shoulder. He was protecting me. Again."

Ward put a steadying hand on her shoulder. "Hey, he'll be fine. He's been through worse."

"So he keeps telling me," she said, forcing a smile.

Before Ward could respond, a doctor came down the hall. He stopped in front of her. "You're Mr. Hoyt's fiancee?" he asked.

She nodded, ignoring Ward's narrowed eyes.

"He's in recovery. You can see him now. Follow me and I'll show you to his room."

"I'll explain later," she said over her shoulder to Ward.

The doctor led her down the hallway. "Maybe you can try to keep your future husband out of the hospital for a while."

She laughed. "I will certainly try," she said as she opened the door.

As much as she hated seeing Hoyt lying in a hospital bed again, this time with a bandage across his shoulder, just below the old scar, she let the joy of seeing him awake and alert and *alive* surge through her as she rushed towards his bed.

"Did you get him?" he asked.

She nodded, trying to hold back the tears.

"Knew you would," he said, his eyes starting to drift shut.

She moved closer, sat down on the edge of his bed, and ran a hand down the side of his face. "I love you."

He smiled, eyes closed. "Love you. Can't die before I put a ring on your finger."

She laughed, then leaned down and kissed him as he fell asleep.

WARD PAUSED outside Hoyt's hospital room. Through the small window he could see Agent Nobles curled up halfway in a chair, half on Agent Hoyt's bed, her hand intertwined with Hoyt's.

He smiled and backed away from the door. Any official business he had with them could wait until the morning.

The real world would intrude all too soon on their peaceful moment. He would let them enjoy it as long as possible.

He hoped like hell they got the chance to see what was developing between them. They certainly deserved it.

He fought down a tiny wave of jealousy as he headed out of the hospital parking lot towards the fast food dinner and empty hotel bed that awaited him.

24

Ang had slept fitfully in the uncomfortable chair next to Hoyt's bed. Her eyes jerked open at a knock on the door early the next morning.

Hoyt pushed himself up to a sitting position as the door opened. "Shit," he muttered when he saw who was entering his room. "What the hell are you doing here?" he asked.

"Nice to see you too, you son of a bitch," the man said, stepping into the room.

Ang recognized the actor instantly. Though he was just as impressive in person as he was on the big screen, he had nothing on John Hoyt in her opinion.

He gave her a lopsided grin. "You must be Special Agent Angelina Nobles," he said in a delicious Irish brogue. "Lash Brogan, at your service," he said, taking her hand in a firm grip.

She nodded, not sure what to say.

A beautiful, dark-haired woman came into the room next, making Lash's entire face light up. "My wife, Lauren Calhoun," he said, pulling her close to him.

Lauren smiled and extended her hand. "I hear you've had the pleasure of working with my asshole older brother."

Ang laughed, instantly liking them both. "I have."

Lash turned back towards Hoyt's bed and frowned down at him. "What are you, a damned bullet magnet?"

Hoyt thought about Ang and smiled. Knew it was worth any amount of pain knowing she was safe and his.

"Now if he'd just stop putting himself in the line of fire," Ang said with a smile.

Lash shook his head. "I don't think that goofy grin on his face is because of the pain meds." He paused, shook his head again. "I never thought I'd see it. John Hoyt in love."

"Oh, he fought it tooth and nail. We both did for a while, but I won him over eventually," Ang said, beaming.

"Well, you got a good man. I owe John a lot." Lash paused and flashed his famous crooked grin. "But he owes me a lot, too. If it hadn't been for me getting into so much damned trouble, he never would have met Ward, and instead of being a big, badass FBI agent, he'd still be a lowly bodyguard."

"I am still here," Hoyt said. "The least you could do is talk about me outside my room."

Ang made her way to his bed, took his hand in hers.

The door opened again, and Ward entered. He shook hands with Lash, hugged his sister. Then he looked from Ang to Hoyt and back to Ang, eyes narrowed.

Ang's face felt warm under his scrutiny. She had yet to explain the whole fiancee thing to her boss. And she really didn't want to do it with a crowd of people around her. But she turned and faced her boss. She opened her mouth, but no words came out.

"Oh, for God's sake," Hoyt said from his hospital bed. "I really didn't want to make this announcement lying on my back in a damned hospital bed, but I asked Ang to marry me." He paused, his voice softening as he looked at her. "And miracle of miracles, she said yes."

Lash gave a whoop of delight and Lauren quickly pulled Ang in for a hug. Ward laughed and shook his head. "Glad you two finally made it official," he said.

Ang sat on the side of Hoyt's bed. He'd never admit it, but she could tell he was in pain and all the activity in his room had exhausted him. "Now, if you'll excuse us, I'd like some time alone with my fiancé."

After a few more minutes of congratulations and hugs, they were left blissfully alone.

"Thank you," Hoyt said.

She looked at him. "For what?"

"For getting everyone the hell out of here." He smiled up at her. "You always seem to know exactly what I need. Even when I don't."

She smiled down at him. "Get used to it."

Hoyt squeezed her hand, fighting the pull of fatigue and the drugs, struggling to keep his eyes open. There was so much he wanted to say to her. Ang kissed his forehead. "Rest, I'm not going anywhere."

He sighed and smiled, letting sleep take him, and despite being shot again, feeling happier than he could ever remember being.

HOYT WAS out of bed early the next morning, ready to get the hell out of the hospital. The pain in his shoulder was down to a dull ache, thanks to the painkillers he'd reluctantly taken earlier. Ang would be there any minute and he was very much looking forward to leaving Casper, WY in the rearview mirror.

And spending some quality time alone with Ang.

He straightened at a knock on his door. It took him a minute to recognize the man walking into his room.

"Paul?" he asked in disbelief.

His informant had shaved and cleaned up dramatically since the last time he saw him bleeding out in the alley.

Paul stepped forward, extended his hand. "I wanted to thank you for saving my life," he said

Hoyt shook his hand. "No thanks necessary. Good to see you on your feet."

"You, too." Paul paused. "Seriously, what happened the other night, almost dying, it was one hell of a wake up call. I haven't had a drink since then and I don't plan to. I've been given another chance at life and I'm not going to fuck it up."

"That's good to hear, man," Hoyt said.

Paul smiled. "I imagine you have a certain woman on her way to pick you up."

Hoyt smiled back. "I do. And I don't intend to fuck that up, either."

25

How the hell did I ever get so lucky? Hoyt thought a week later as he watched Ang on the couch across the room from him. Sure, he'd served his country. He'd taken bullets protecting someone. More than once. And he was perfectly willing to sacrifice himself again. That he knew.

But being loved was something he didn't know. He'd never known what that felt like before Ang.

She'd been spoiling him rotten since they got back from Casper. She'd insisted on him staying with her while he recovered since her place was bigger and nicer than his sparsely furnished bachelor apartment. She'd painstakingly taken care of checking and re-bandaging his wound. She'd even cooked for him. And she was a damned good cook. That had been a nice surprise.

And he had to admit, it was nice, being looked after. But he was ready to turn that around and take care of her.

He picked up the remote control and turned off the TV. Ang raised her head out of the mystery novel she was reading. "Ready for bed?" she asked.

"Oh, yes," he answered, standing and stalking towards her.

He enjoyed the surprised yelp she made as he gripped her knees and pulled her towards him.

She smiled, feeling his hardness against her core, wrapping her legs tightly around his waist.

He pulled her closer, kissing her long and deep.

She pulled back, breathing hard. "Are you sure your shoulder is okay?"

"Baby, I don't give a damn if I bleed out as long as I'm inside you."

"Not funny," she replied, but she was smiling.

"I'd carry you into the bedroom, but that might not be the best idea right now. But if you can manage to walk there, I'll make it worth your while."

He stepped back and she stood, taking his hand. "I'll hold you to that," she said, leading him down the hall.

THREE DAYS LATER, Ward studied his two agents as they sat in front of his desk. Ang now had a diamond ring on her left hand and seemed to be glowing. Hoyt still moved a little stiffly and his face was a touch paler than normal, but he looked happier and more content than Ward had ever seen him. It was quite the opposite dynamic than what he'd witnessed during their first meeting in his office.

He chuckled and shook his head.

"What?" Hoyt asked.

"Just thinking about my second career as a matchmaker."

ABOUT THE AUTHOR

Originally from Kansas, Sara Vinduska is a romantic suspense author and aspiring farmer in Wyoming. Her other passions include yoga, soap making, good red wine, and K-State football.

ALSO BY SARA VINDUSKA

The Drowning Man

Reflections (Fateful Justice Book 1)

Redemption (Fateful Justice Book 2)

COMING SOON: RECLAIMED (FATEFUL JUSTICE BOOK 4)

Chapter 1

Mark Goddard knew he was riding sloppy, wasn't surprised at all when the bucking bull got the best of him and he went flying through the air.

He hit the ground hard, flat on his back. The air whooshed out of his lungs and the entire back side of his body exploded in pain. He tried to take a breath, but his lungs refused to work. He tried again.

Nothing.

Panic started. God, he was going to die right here in the dirt. He couldn't move, couldn't breathe. His vision dimmed. Reality merged with the past. He was trapped inside the pitch black trunk of a car, dying, drowning in his own blood.

Voices came from somewhere above him. Then a hand was on his shoulder, squeezing gently.

Not alone.

His lungs finally decided to get with the program and he gasped in air. His vision cleared. He could see his mentor, Rodney, squatted down next to him, could see the bottom of the arena fence. Smell the dirt and the animals. Hear the roar of the crowd.

Not in the trunk.

He closed his eyes. Breathed.

"Can you move?" Rodney asked.

He opened his eyes again. "Let's find out."

He looked around. The bull was safely back in the chutes. His buddy Lane, one of the two bullfighters in the arena, was looking at him, concern etched on his face.

Rodney helped him to his feet. Mark wavered on shaky legs, managed a wave at the roaring crowd, let the older man lead him out of the arena.

"Damn, boy, let's get you checked out," Rodney said, heading towards the medic tent.

Mark stopped and shook his head. "Nah. I'm okay."

Rodney looked him up and down. "You hit pretty damned hard."

Mark rolled his shoulders. "Nothing's broken, just sore. We both know I've had wrecks way worse than that."

Rodney shrugged. No point in arguing. The stupid, stubborn SOB.

"Just need a few drinks and maybe some female company, I'll be good as new," Mark said with a wink.

"Okay," Rodney answered, wishing not for the first time that the young man he considered a son wasn't so hell bent on self-destruction.

Mark turned back towards the arena in time to see the last rider get bucked off his bull and scramble over the fence to safety. "Guess that's it for the night," he said to Rodney, then made his way to where the other riders were gathering.

"You okay?" his buddy Lane asked, still dressed in his bull fighter costume.

"I'm good," Mark answered. "Ready for a drink."

"If you're sure," Lane said, not looking convinced.

"Damn sure." The last thing Mark wanted right now was to be alone. Not yet. Not with the memories so close to the surface.

So he followed Lane and several of the other riders to Misfits, their usual hangout. He ordered a beer and a shot of bourbon, started to feel the pain in his back receding. Then he kept drinking. Drank until the memories faded, until he didn't hurt at all.

The alcohol might have dulled the physical pain, but not the dark thoughts swirling around in his head. There wasn't enough alcohol in the world to erase those.

He knew how inconsistent his riding had been lately. When he was on, he was on. When he wasn't, he was damned lucky he hadn't gotten himself seriously injured or worse. He knew it pissed Rodney off to no end that he was wasting his natural God-given talent.

Lane turned towards him, looking unsteady on his bar stool. "Shit, I'm fucked up, man. How you doin'?"

"I'm good," Mark lied, not wanting to talk about what was going on in his head. Not even with Lane.

Lane was the best damned bullfighter he'd ever met. And one of the best men he'd ever had the privilege of being friends with. Though he was named after a famous bull rider, Lane had taken the art of bullfighting to a whole new level. He was amazing to watch in action and had saved Mark's ass on numerous occasions. Including tonight.

"Can I tell you something?" Lane asked, slightly slurring his words.

Mark knew he wasn't going to like whatever it was his friend had to say, but he was drunk enough that he didn't give a shit. "Say it."

Lane looked him in the eyes. "You're the best bull rider I've ever seen, no doubt in my mind, but if your heart's not in it anymore, I'd rather see you quit than get yourself killed."

The words cut through the drunken fog in Mark's head. Lane was right. He should honor his commitments and sponsorships then get the hell out while he still could.

And then what?

That was the million dollar question. What the hell did he do if he didn't ride bulls?

He took another drink.

He needed something to focus on, or he'd fall right back down into the pit of darkness and depression he'd struggled so damned hard to get out of. And even now, he felt like he was hanging onto the edge with his fingertips.

No one is safe.

The words echoed in his head. But he refused to give in to the memories.

He ran a hand down his face. Somehow he needed to get his shit together.

But not tonight, he thought as he finished his drink and looked around the room at the women gathered around the bar in various states of dress and drunkenness. His eyes settled on a dark-haired beauty in a tight red tank top.

Tonight he was going to get blind stinking drunk and fuck a beautiful woman.

Dubois, Wyoming Sheriff Lieutenant Whitney York let herself into her hotel room and sighed. She looked around the small space that was her temporary home. She'd been looking at the same bland room for the past two months. *God, had it really been that long?*

She'd left almost everything she owned in storage back in Raleigh when she'd moved. *Or ran away,* her mind added.

She put her purse and bag of food down on the desk and went into the bathroom to wash her hands, carefully avoiding looking at herself in the mirror.

She seemed to be doing that a lot lately.

She'd settled into a daily routine of getting coffee at the small stand down the block from the hotel, going to work, then eating a take-out dinner back in her room while she watched the evening news.

In some ways, the boring routine was nice. The Fremont County Sheriff's office was a far cry from what she'd seen daily as a detective in Raleigh, NC. Not much crime to deal with here in the small town of around 1,000 people and that suited her just fine. Her co-workers were nice and had finally stopped trying to get her to go out with them after work.

They were all decent people and seemed to be competent at what they did. She just had no interest in getting friendly with any of them. It just wasn't worth the effort. Not that she had the energy or desire to put forth much effort into building relationships. Maybe someday. But not right now.

But she couldn't shake the feeling of being in limbo. Hadn't even bothered to look for an apartment to rent, much less a house to buy.

The thought of returning to Raleigh for her things made her physically sick. She had to find a way to move forward, she knew that.

But not tonight, she thought as she settled in to watch a chick flick movie on HBO while eating Chinese take out.

Made in the USA
Las Vegas, NV
12 December 2022

62209095R00114